Room 46

Helen McKenna

Room 46

By Helen McKenna

Printed in Australia by Lightning Source
Cover design by Younique Creation

ISBN 13: 9780992436391

Website: www.helenmckenna.com.au

Email: info@helenmckenna.com.au

For Belle-Marie,

Who taught me there is no age barrier to

friendship…

Prologue

It took several attempts to force her eyes open.

Edith couldn't understand why it was proving so difficult. Blinking was an instinctive action so how could something so simple take so much effort? But then again she had never felt this weak in her life.

When she finally convinced her eyelids to lift Edith immediately realised why her brain had resisted. The lights in the room were far too bright, and the nurse's uniform so white it gave her an instant headache. The signs on the wall seemed to be in a foreign language. And the voices she could hear were also alien; she couldn't comprehend a single word.

Joe. Where was Joe?

Using all her strength she tried to vocalise her husband's name but the sound simply wouldn't come. She couldn't even move her lips into the right position to speak.

He must be somewhere close by. She had just been speaking to him, hadn't she? Yes she had, and he had told her to hang on and that she was going to be all right. But if she had spoken only moments ago, why couldn't she now? It couldn't have been a dream, surely? It was too real, too vivid.

It took a moment for the horrible memories to filter back. Then the realisation hit. Joe was dead. And she was all alone in some strange hospital literally feeling the last vestiges of life drain from her broken body.

Edith wanted to hang on like Joe had asked her to but she didn't have the strength. Despite doing her best to stay awake, her eyes fluttered closed without the nurse even realising they had been open, and she drifted back into the void.

Marion

People were always surprised when Marion said she loved her job. She wasn't sure why a cleaner couldn't be as fulfilled by their work as say a teacher or an engineer, but if popular opinion was anything to go by then apparently you couldn't. It seemed that everyone thought you only went into cleaning as a last resort and got out as soon as something better turned up. But that was certainly not the case for Marion.

Over the years she had worked in many different places – office buildings, educational institutions, hospitals and even in a prison at one time – but Rosehill Gardens was her favourite. Even though her friends had warned it might make her depressed Marion found the opposite to be true. She learned so much from the residents and loved the joy she could bring to them by such simple things as dusting bookshelves and mopping the floor.

The best thing about Rosehill was being paid by the room and not the hour, leaving each individual to choose the pace at which they worked. Marion had been cleaning long enough to do the job very efficiently but had also worked out the perfect pace to appear busy but still have a great chat in each room. Her only previous complaint about her career as a cleaner had been the lack of human contact given that most cleaners appeared when the workers left. Being a sociable person, she couldn't believe her luck when she landed the Rosehill gig and found out conversation was actually encouraged.

Marion tried to explain her system to the other cleaners on the roster but none of them could see the sense in it. Zindzi the uni student preferred to creep in early and get the job done before any of the residents were awake. An overachiever all her life, she had two other part time jobs and held the record for the fastest average time per room.

A former bodybuilder who still hit the gym every day, Matheus took pride in being imposing and boasted that almost all the residents he cleaned for found a reason to leave their room whenever he appeared with his trolley. His appearance alone was enough to discourage conversation.

And then there was Hazel who had such a gloomy outlook on life that she barely saw the point in cleaning at all when things would only get dirty again. Privately, Marion suspected that the residents just put up with her barely acceptable surface cleans rather than have to deal with the negative energy she exuded any longer than absolutely necessary.

In the end Marion gave up on all attempts to convert others to her system and went about her business in her own way. A stellar performance review after her probation period convinced her that she was doing a great job.

Marion's spinster great aunt had been the one to bestow upon her what she considered to be one of life's great pearls of wisdom. Picking up on Marion's frustration that her mother wouldn't let her make her own choices, Auntie Flo had invited her out for tea in a fancy hotel one afternoon in a time before there was a coffee shop on every corner.

'You remind me of myself,' Auntie Flo confided, as she sipped her tea with her little finger properly extended.

Doing her best not to look offended, Marion snuck a glance at the elegant woman sitting opposite, who was as straight laced as they came and frowned upon any kind of misbehaviour. As a teenager living in the free-wheeling seventies it was not a comparison Marion welcomed.

Still, she had been taught to respect her elders and managed a polite smile. 'Really?' she asked. 'In what way?'

'You like to think outside the square and move to the beat of your own drum.'

Marion had to agree this was true.

'The key to going against the status quo without upsetting people is to make them think that whatever you want to do is *their* idea. Then they won't put up barriers to stop you reaching your goal.'

Marion laughed. 'I don't think Mum will ever believe that me buying a crochet bikini or being allowed to smoke in the house is *her* idea.'

Surprisingly Auntie Flo laughed too. 'Well, no, it doesn't work in every case,' she agreed. 'But for most situations if you think about it first and put some subtle ground work in you'll be surprised just how many things go your way.'

Auntie Flo's words had proven to be true. Desperate to escape her parents' dream of a job in a bank Marion had instead applied for a cleaning job at the airport. Having oh so casually mentioned many weeks earlier how airline employees got free flights, her mother had beamed at the news.

'Didn't I tell you Marion that you have to start from the ground up? Once you get your foot in the door you'll be able to get any job you want out there!'

Marion didn't bother to explain that she already had the job she wanted but it bought her the time to get established and prove she was happy in her work. By then her mother had turned her attention to her younger sister and never questioned Marion's career choice again.

As her life progressed she continued to use the technique and more often than not she got what she wanted. Nobody could believe it when free spirited Gary presented her with an engagement ring at a time when marriage was distinctly unfashionable. Nor could they fathom how Marion convinced him to exchange his somewhat dubious career as a used car salesman for an apprenticeship as a mechanic.

The most delicate negotiations to date had concerned her daughter Ellie. Terrified at the prospect of the teenager spending her gap year roaming around Europe without so much as a pre-paid train ticket, Marion had managed to convince Ellie to restructure her plans to include several Contiki tours interspersed with an Au Pair job in Cambridge.

After that had come off Gary had stared at her in amazement. 'I'm really not sure how you did that,' he stated somewhat suspiciously and for a moment Marion had panicked, scared that he might start second guessing their life together. 'I'm glad you did though,' he added, relief evident in his tone.

* * * * *

Assistant Manager Sylvia Jenkins was running late the morning Marion came across the official paperwork on her desk at Rosehill Gardens. Scanning the file Marion's eyes grew wide and in that moment she knew it was up to her to make sure this proposal came to fruition. She had heard

Sylvia debating the issue on the phone the week before and knew she was in two minds about taking it on.

'There's so much paperwork,' she had said to her friend Libby, who worked at Centrelink. 'And I'd feel bad if it didn't work out. It's a big responsibility and you know me, I'd rather not do it at all than do it half-heartedly.'

By the time Sylvia arrived Marion had the office spic and span and a mug of steaming hot chai tea ready on the desk. People were always more receptive to ideas when they weren't flustered. She reassured Sylvia that the clock on the wall was three minutes fast and insisted she take a moment to get settled before she started her busy day.

'Thanks Marion I think I might,' Sylvia agreed, picking up her mug and taking a welcoming sip.

As Marion packed up her gear she told Sylvia about the report she had just heard on the radio about the new welfare rules. 'They were interviewing a young lass about a special program she'd been in,' Marion mentioned casually as she arranged the contents of her cleaning cart just so. 'Reborn or re-grow or something…'

'Rejoin,' Sylvia murmured.

'Yes, that's it. Anyway she said how it had literally transformed her life! She couldn't say enough good things about it.'

'Hmmm that's interesting,' Sylvia said, turning her chair to look out the window.

Although pretending not to notice, as she backed out the door Marion saw Sylvia pick up the paperwork and look at it thoughtfully.

Grace

As nursing homes went it was a nice one, far better than Grace had expected. Radiating from a central entrance hub the low set brick building expanded symmetrically east and west and was surrounded by eucalypts, bottlebrush trees and a colourful display of gerberas and impatiens. A simple but striking water feature in the centre of the main garden bubbled softly over smooth pebbles as a chorus of birdsong sounded in the background like a nature CD.

Locking her ancient Hyundai Excel with the key Grace took a deep breath and made her way across the car park. It didn't take long to find the front office and once she introduced herself Grace was ushered into a nearby office by the sharp featured woman on reception. 'Sylvia will be with you in a moment,' she announced briskly.

Grace nodded and took a seat, not really caring how long Sylvia took. It wasn't as if she had anything better to do with her morning.

As it happened she didn't need to wait long. Dressed in tailored slacks and a pale pink linen shirt, Sylvia was much younger than Grace had anticipated, probably only ten years older than she was. Anxiety gripped Grace. What would this professional woman think of her? Would she question why she was volunteering in a nursing home instead of working in a normal job like other people her age?

'Hello, Grace is it?'

'Yes that's right,' Grace murmured eyes downcast.

Sylvia held out her hand. 'Welcome to Rosehill Gardens. I'm Sylvia Jenkins, Assistant Manager and volunteer co-ordinator.'

Grace returned the handshake and managed a strained smile.

Settling herself at the desk Sylvia flipped open a manila file and sorted through the paperwork inside. Grace could see a referral letter from Centrelink as well as a report from the Mental Health Accessibility Centre. Heat flushed her neck and cheeks, then prickled her scalp. Wasn't anything private anymore? Her past experiences should be confidential, not shared with random strangers who knew nothing about her.

'Right then,' Sylvia began, her eyes still on the paperwork in front of her. 'I see you're on the Rejoin Program?'

'Yes, that's correct.' Grace studied Sylvia's face for the usual signs of pity or scorn that sometimes greeted this information, but saw neither. Apparently she was one of those bleeding heart types who genuinely believed in such programs, or she just didn't care. Grace wasn't sure which she preferred. It didn't matter what anybody said, mental health issues still carried a stigma that was impossible to escape, especially if you wanted to keep collecting a disability pension. Everybody was applauding the federal minister's shake-up of the welfare rules but all they could see were the cost savings. They just didn't understand that some people – like her – would never be able to hold down a normal job. She had no choice but to go through the motions of completing the program even knowing as she did that it was a complete waste of time.

'Okay Grace, this all looks in order,' Sylvia said, writing some notes in the file before snapping it closed and sliding it across to the left edge of the desk. Lacing her fingers together she sat up straight and looked over at her newest volunteer in a way that Grace couldn't quite decipher.

Kindness? Curiosity?

Grace met her eyes briefly before shifting her gaze back down to the desktop.

'Tell me, why did you choose a nursing home for your placement?'

Grace hesitated. She didn't imagine Sylvia would want to hear that it seemed like the easiest choice from the options offered to her. Really, how hard could it be to sit and talk to a bedridden person? It had to be much less confronting than interacting with the public in an op shop or having to deal with hordes of kids in a day care centre.

'Uh, I understand the concept of loneliness,' she said finally. 'I know lots of nursing home residents are alone so I thought having someone to talk to might help.'

Sylvia nodded thoughtfully. 'Okay then, that's good, very good. I'm sure you'll be able to make a big contribution here at Rosehill Gardens.'

With the paperwork sorted out, Sylvia escorted Grace past the main dining area and sitting room, chatting easily as they walked. 'It really is a lovely facility,' she said, nodding and smiling at a nurse as she hurried past and stepping aside to let a tiny, birdlike woman hunched over a walking frame shuffle across the hallway into the library.

Grace nodded. It did seem to be a nice place. Although fairly basic in design, it was a modern building that was well maintained. It was also free from that overwhelming stench of disinfectant she remembered from the place her Great Aunt Mavis used to live.

Heading off down one of the main hallways, Grace tried not to stare as they walked past the open doorways of residents' rooms. She shuddered a little as she caught a glimpse of a shrivelled looking man trying to reposition his wheelchair so he could see the TV better. Both his legs were amputated below the knee. He seemed so small, so insignificant. Grace shuddered again, realising that this could well be her fate in another fifty or sixty years, alone in a nursing home with no family or friends to visit.

Realising she was getting worked up, Grace focused on her breathing. In and out, she repeated to herself, in and out.

They rounded another corner and Sylvia led Grace into a small alcove near the nurses' station. 'Righto, we've got you visiting Edith. She's an amazing woman with a great spirit despite all her health problems. She inspires the staff here every day by just being herself.'

'Really?' Grace's case worker had given her a brief rundown on Edith and while Grace realised she wasn't a typical nursing home patient, she hadn't expected her to be the star of the place.

'Absolutely. Edith and her husband Joe were on a trip around Australia when they were involved in a horrific car accident. Joe died at the scene but Edith survived against all odds. She spent six months in hospital and another five months in rehab. Having just re-learned how to walk, she was preparing to finally go home when a dormant blood clot caused a major stroke that paralysed her entire left side. Sadly there was no other option but full time care.'

'Oh. That's so sad.'

'Yes, sadder than average, that's for sure. You can't keep Edith down though. Until a few weeks ago she was talking about getting back on the grey nomad trail.'

'Grey nomad trail?' Grace said. 'But isn't she …?'

Sylvia nodded. 'Yes it was a bit of a pipe dream. And sadly she has suffered a fairly major setback since then.'

'Setback?'

'Yes, Edith suffered another stroke six weeks ago. Devastatingly this one has knocked out her speech, which has been a huge upheaval not just for her but for us as well. We all loved talking to Edith,' she murmured fondly, her eyes misting over just for second. 'She was one of those people who could really carry a great conversation.'

This piece of information gave Grace pause and she eyed Sylvia quizzically.

Sylvia met her gaze. 'I know what you're thinking – why bother? What's the point of visiting someone who can't speak back to you?'

Grace's cheeks reddened. 'Uh no, um well, I'm not much of a talker. I thought I would just be replying to what Edith wanted to chat about.'

'Sure, some of our residents are like that, but having read your case notes we thought Edith would be a good match for you.'

Mortified that her life had been laid bare for strangers to make decisions about, Grace flushed again.

'There's your age too,' Sylvia added. 'Edith loves having young visitors and most of our volunteers are older. And despite the latest stroke Edith is still very much her old self underneath.'

'So is there any chance she will improve?'

'It's not sounding too hopeful. She's diligently undertaking all the physical therapy but the brain scans show some pretty devastating damage and because there were still residual deficits, the doctors just don't know if it can be reversed.'

Seeds of uncertainty began to bud in Grace's gut. By all accounts Edith was some kind of living legend, who despite all that she had endured was still positive and full of life. And she, well she wasn't a typical twenty year old and would be able to offer little in the way of youthful optimism to someone with such a tragic life.

'So what do I talk about then?' she asked, desperation obvious in her voice.

'Don't panic Grace,' Sylvia reassured her kindly. 'Edith used to be an English teacher. She really enjoys being read to and then for you to give your opinion about the story. There's a book in her bedside locker.'

'Okay,' Grace replied, her calm tone belying the churning in her stomach.

'Just relax and don't focus her physical state. Although her body has broken down her mind is still functioning.'

'Right,' Grace said, her mind awash with questions but unable to articulate any of them.

'She really didn't want to move in here,' Sylvia said as they walked along, 'and all things being fair she shouldn't have had to.'

'Well, I don't suppose anybody really wants to move into a nursing home.'

Sylvia nodded and chuckled softly. 'Yes, you're right about that Grace. As nice as we try to make them, they are not on anybody's wish list of places to live. But sadly Edith has no extended family which meant no other means of care.'

'Oh, that's unusual,' Grace said, feeling she should

make some contribution to the conversation. 'She doesn't have children of her own then?'

'No, sadly she doesn't.'

Sylvia started walking again, pausing outside a door with the number 46 painted on it in a fancy font. 'I'll just go in and let her know you're here,' she explained, 'and then you can go in and introduce yourself.'

Sylvia disappeared inside the room and Grace seriously considered making a quick exit. This was all too difficult, too confronting. She didn't know anything about people in nursing homes. As a child she had hated those duty visits to Great Aunt Mavis, and had counted the minutes until they could leave while her parents and siblings had seemed totally comfortable with it all. It had been more than ten years since she died and Grace had never been inside a nursing home since.

If she hurried now she could make a getaway. Yes, she would have some explaining to do with her case worker, but surely anything was better than this horrible uncertainty that was building within her. Had Sylvia not emerged right at that moment and motioned her into the room, Grace knew she would have run back along the maze of hallways and out the front door.

* * * * *

It took Grace's eyes a moment to adjust to the riot of colour. Far from the starkness of the rooms she had glimpsed along the hallway, Edith's room featured the brightest shades on the Dulux colour chart. A wardrobe of electric blue and a vibrant aqua bedside locker contrasted with deep crimson walls, one of which was adorned with a butterfly mural painted in the brightest fluorescent colours Grace had even seen. Lying supported on a nest of candy striped pillows and a matching doona, Edith herself was dressed in a hot pink bed jacket.

Grace tried to avert her eyes from the wheelchair and the other medical equipment in the room, but it was impossible not to stare just a bit. It was hard to comprehend that this room was Edith's reality for however much longer she might live.

Like the other people she had encountered at Rosehill Gardens so far, Edith seemed tiny and shrunken. Although difficult to estimate a person's height when they are lying down, Grace guessed she couldn't be much more than one hundred and sixty centimetres tall. And Edith's slight body hardly made an impression in the bedclothes. Her hair was another story. Rich plum waves tumbled down her shoulders, putting Grace's mousey brown ponytail to shame. Was it a wig? Or extensions? Surely the staff of the facility did not have time to style a resident's hair every day?

Paralysed by the horrible yet familiar anxiety she had come to know so well, Grace hovered near the door. This was not going to be as straightforward as she had anticipated. Why had she agreed to open herself up to scrutiny? To the possibility of being judged? Why did life have to be so bloody hard?

Edith turned to look at her apparently attempting to smile as much as the drooping muscles in her face allowed.

Smiling politely in response, Grace suddenly felt awkward standing still and moved towards the foot of the bed. 'Hello I'm Grace,' she said.

Edith continued to look at her intently and blinked slowly and deliberately.

Grace smiled back uncertainly. No doubt the blink meant something, but how was she supposed to know what? Why hadn't she asked Sylvia how to communicate? Shame prickled her conscience as she acknowledged that she had assumed the whole visiting thing was going to be simply about sitting next to an old person and listening to them talk for an hour. Clearly it was much more than that.

Looking up at the wall to avoid Edith's continuing gaze, Grace noticed a wedding photo of a younger looking Edith in a delicate lace gown and matching veil. Her groom, much taller and with the freckliest complexion Grace had ever seen, stood proudly beside her. It was hard to match that image with the one before her and she felt a pang in her chest upon realising just what Edith's life had come to as a result of a random accident. It must be the pits to have your whole life reduced to just one room. To have to rely on other people to care for every physical need. To be bedridden twenty-four/seven.

Looking around Grace noticed a recliner chair on the far side of the bed. Covered in a faded plaid fabric, it seemed an odd addition to the room but it was clearly where people sat when they visited. 'May I?' she asked softly.

The blink again, which Grace thought was safe to assume was a yes.

She sat down, immediately sinking low into the sagging springs. Making herself as comfortable as she could, she relaxed a little. Reading she could do. She could rely on somebody else's words instead of having to dredge up her own.

Remembering Sylvia's comment about the book, Grace reached down, struggling at first to get the drawer open. It was crammed full and something was caught that refused to allow it to open more than a few centimetres. Kneeling on the floor, she wedged her fingers into the gap and dislodged the cardboard cover of a writing pad. Once open the drawer revealed a jumbled mess of manila folders, A4 envelopes and old-fashioned stationery sets.

Grace gasped when her hand touched a plastic folder containing a pad of paper with a floral motif on one side and two sets of matching envelopes, each in their own pouch. She couldn't help but run her hands over the cover. 'My grandma had one just like this,' she said. 'We always got her a new one for Christmas each year, always the same pattern. She said it was her favourite.'

Grace wasn't sure but she thought the expression on Edith's face was a smile.

Unable to find a normal paperback Grace extracted a bound A4 sized document with a green back cover and a clear plastic front from the drawer. It was simply entitled "Short Stories". Flipping through it quickly Grace could see it was double spaced with wide margins and printed on one side only. It wasn't terribly thick, perhaps two hundred pages or so. They wouldn't get it all read today, but she could make a dent in it.

Adjusting her position slightly, Edith turned her head a little towards Grace, a movement that clearly took concerted effort.

Grace felt another pang, realising she had never been so affronted by the suffering of another human being.

Opening the plastic cover and flipping through the cover and contents pages, Grace settled back into the sagging springs and began to read.

Josephine Wilson woke before her alarm. She set it religiously every night, just in case she should oversleep. But she never did. An old fashioned blue clock with a silver bell on the top, it was the type that had to be wound each night. This didn't bother Josephine; in fact, it was an integral part of her nightly bedtime ritual. Besides why spend good money on a modern appliance that used power? A few cents a day onto her electricity might not sound like much, but these things all added up over time. No, as long as her clock kept ticking, she would keep using it.

The same applied to her twenty-year-old bed. It was not the most attractive piece of furniture, but it was serviceable and sturdy. And it had a reading lamp built into it. Sure it was quite a narrow single, but who cared? Although her landlord laughed each time he saw it, Josephine had never contemplated getting a new one.

Less than five minutes after waking Josephine was standing under a hot shower, one eye on the Brisbane City Council four minute timer to ensure she kept her gas bill minimal. After drying off and donning her dressing gown Josephine seated herself at the tiny laminex-topped table. She took ten minutes to eat a small bowl of porridge and a piece of wholemeal toast with marmalade, and to clear the table. Getting dressed took only another five minutes as

Josephine's wardrobe was conservative, her hairstyle plain and she wore no makeup. At 7.25 am on the dot she locked her door and set off on foot for the railway station. Josephine had never owned a car and had no plans to buy one.

The train trip to the city took forty-seven minutes which was just enough time to read the paper. As usual Josephine didn't need to buy a copy as there were always so many discarded ones available for the taking. Today she managed to grab the latest *Woman's Day* as well. Glancing at the price on the cover Josephine shuddered. Who would pay that kind of money to read celebrity gossip? Still it was worth a flick through when it was free. She tucked the magazine into her handbag for later and took her usual seat in carriage three.

Josephine had no idea of the amount of conversation she generated amongst the other commuters on the 7.38 am city service. A group of ten or so had banded together over the years and although she had travelled on the same train every day for as long as any of them could remember, Josephine had never made any effort to join in their group. She would reply politely when spoken to but never went beyond the basic pleasantries.

There was a long standing bet with a prize pool of one hundred dollars for anybody who could get Josephine to join one of their card games. Jerry, who worked in a sandwich bar at Central Station, would often have a go at drawing her in. Catching the eye of his fellow commuter Amanda, he sat down beside Josephine and smiled broadly.

'How are you this morning Josephine?' he asked jovially.

'Very well, thank you Jerry. Yourself?'

'I'm fantastic. Can we tempt you to join a hand of gin rummy? Pete is getting a bit cocky and we need a new challenger.'

Josephine shook her head. 'Come on Jerry, I've told you before I'm not one for cards,' she replied and turned her attention back to the paper.

Amanda, who was a teller at Westpac, punched Jerry playfully on the arm as he re-joined her. 'Well done Jez, you're as irresistible as ever.'

'You can't say I don't try.'

In addition to the hundred dollar prize pool, there was a bonus of a further fifty dollars for anybody who could extract some personal information from Josephine. Of particular interest was where she worked. Jerry and Amanda had discussed the possibilities at great length but still had no idea. When asked where she worked, Josephine would answer, 'In the city'.

One morning Amanda had pressed her further by asking, 'Where in the city?', to which Josephine had replied, 'In Queen Street'. Her tone and body language had conveyed that no further questions would be answered.

'So do you still think she's a nun?' Jerry asked as he rummaged in his backpack for a stick of chewing gum.

'It's quite possible you know,' said Amanda. 'They don't wear the habit and veil any more, they just have to dress conservatively, which she definitely does. It would explain her reluctance to talk about herself and what she does.

31

Aren't nuns supposed to keep their good works to themselves?'

'I suppose so. But what good works could she be doing in Queen Street? Besides I saw a *Woman's Day* in her bag. Do you think a nun would read that?'

'She might be visiting a sick person in hospital and taking some reading material.'

'In between her other good works you mean?'

Amanda put her hand out for a piece of gum. 'Scoff all you like but nobody else has come up with a better answer yet, have they? Besides no woman I know would wear such hideous shoes without good reason. I don't even know where you can buy such fashion disasters.'

Jerry laughed. 'You and your shoes. Somebody should tail her one day.'

'Have you seen how fast she walks? She's the first one out of the train and is long gone by the time anybody else even gets to the escalator.'

To illustrate her point Amanda tilted her head towards the nearest door where Josephine was standing ready and waiting to exit, even though there were three more stops before they reached Central Station.

The walk from the train station to her office took ten minutes, although Josephine could manage it in eight if she hurried. Today the train was on time, so she walked at a steady pace and arrived unflustered. She had worked at Blackstone Imports/Exports for the past decade. The previous fifteen years had been spent in a similar job at JTJ Building Industries.

A large company with a multi-million dollar annual turnover, Blackstone was not shy about advertising its affluence. The office furnishings were showy and opulent, the staffing ratio was more than generous and the technology, working conditions and salary packages were way above industry standard. Positions at Blackstone were highly sought after.

Josephine nodded briefly at the clique of employees gossiping in the foyer before heading straight for the lift but shook her head disapprovingly at the same group as she waited for the car to reach the ground floor. In her opinion there was far too much time wasted on idle chit chat in this company.

Wendy, the human resources manager, made a gagging noise after Josephine walked past. 'Another stunningly cutting edge outfit from Josie's collection. Is it just me or can you detect the lingering smell of moth balls?'

Nicki from Accounts laughed. 'She's obviously working on the theory that if you keep something long enough it will come back into fashion.'

'She came to see me the other day about a problem with her pay and told me that long nails were impractical for typing. If Mr Green hadn't been standing nearby I would have really let her have it. Stupid old biddy.' Wendy picked a small piece of lint off her elegant charcoal Cue suit and examined the glossy red finish of her newly applied acrylic nails.

Following suit, Nicki examined her own nails and frowned at the chipped pink polish on her left pinkie. 'How old is she anyway? Fifty or maybe even sixty?'

33

'She acts like she's seventy,' Wendy replied. 'But I'll have a peek at her personnel file and let you know.'

Meanwhile, Josephine was walking briskly along the corridor of the second floor, heading for the kitchen. After putting her lunch in the fridge and her handbag in her locker, she removed a notebook from her pocket and made some notes, careful that she was still on her own time.

At 8.45 am on the dot she removed her jacket and started her day's work.

Ten minutes later, Wendy emailed Nicki revealing that Josephine was in fact forty-six years old.

At 9.45 am, Josephine made her first rounds of the day with the tea trolley. Understanding that her role was to be of service – yet to remain very much in the background – she did not initiate small talk, but responded politely if any of the staff engaged with her. But with the two stops at the end offices there was no chance of that so Josephine would always start with those to get the worst out of the way first.

'Watch those papers!' Senior Manager Gerald Pitts snapped as she picked up the teapot. 'That's a million dollar contract you're about to slop tea on.'

He returned to his phone conversation, but hawk-like watched her every move. Josephine carefully placed his tea and biscuits on the corner of his antique silky oak desk and left the room without a word.

Her second stop, Frank Pearson ignored her all together, his eyes never leaving the documents he was reading. But when Josephine went to set down his special blend Darjeeling and fruit cake on the desk he shook his head and pointed to the other end of the table. It was a little charade he insisted on continuing. When he was in a particularly nasty mood Frank would "accidentally" knock his morning tea onto the floor and have his secretary order Josephine to clean it up. Sometimes it would take several applications of stain remover to clean the luxurious, deep pile carpet. Yet Josephine never reacted in any way. Frank's mind games had little effect on her.

Managing Director David Green was much more courteous. 'Ah Josephine, right on cue as always. I'm dying for my coffee. How are you this fine morning?'

'I'm well thank you Mr Green. We've got chocolate, cream or plain biscuits today, which would you fancy?'

'I'll take the plain thanks. I haven't been near the gym in weeks and it's starting to show,' David said, patting his stomach.

Josephine set the cup, saucer and plate down and nodded politely before pushing her trolley silently out of the office. David rested his feet on his open lower desk drawer and sipped his coffee. As managing director he knew what tea ladies earned and couldn't fathom why anyone would slave away each day for such a pittance. He often wondered why Josephine didn't do a secretarial course and move up in the world. Despite being a bit odd, she was intelligent and courteous. She was capable of far more than her lowly tea lady position.

He was aware of the speculation and decidedly unkind gossip about Josephine around the office. The younger women made fun of her plain appearance, unfashionable clothes and stern manner. And the men joked about the state of her love life. A true gentleman, David refused to contribute to these conversations, but he had to agree with some of the issues raised. Josephine never attended social functions and was not a member of the social club. She refused to contribute to collections for presents or for the Friday Wine Fund.

Even so, David defended her when the other staff complained about her stinginess. He pointed out that it couldn't be easy to live on such a small salary and that Josephine might even be supporting an elderly parent or have some heavy financial commitments. But his comments had little impact and David couldn't help but think that with just a little bit more effort Josephine could fit in much better.

She didn't seem to want to though.

Hardly any of the young secretaries ordered from the tea trolley. Most of them preferred to slip down to Fi Fi's Café for one of the more exotic – and in Josephine's opinion highly overpriced – brews on offer there. Therefore, more than half the desks were empty when Josephine made her rounds through the secretarial pool at 10.35. It didn't escape her attention that the trip to the cafe would increase morning tea breaks from the regulation fifteen minutes to half an hour. As she held no sway in office politics, Josephine didn't voluntarily offer her opinions to anyone, but if anybody cared to ask she could report the movements of most of the staff in the office.

She noticed many other things too like how much stationary was pilfered. Today she had watched Brad furtively slip a stapler, a box of staples and a couple of USB drives into his briefcase, whereas Tina didn't seem to care who noticed her depositing in her handbag two notebooks, a handful of pens and a bulky sticky tape dispenser with a backup roll. Meanwhile, Catriona had been giggling and cooing like a lovebird into her work phone for the last twenty minutes and Josephine knew that Catriona's boyfriend was currently working in Perth. Then again Catriona's boss, Jayne spent an excessive amount of time making her own personal long distance phone calls, so she was unlikely to call Catriona out on her behaviour.

Furthermore Josephine couldn't believe how unproductive some of the staff were. Colin O'Brien was renowned for having the cleanest desktop in the building and everybody agreed that was because so little work was performed on it. Josephine couldn't fathom why nobody confronted him about it.

Making her way through the Accounts section Josephine shook her head at the recently installed widescreen, super-slim monitors on each desk. Out of curiosity she had priced them and couldn't believe the company had wasted so much money replacing monitors that still worked. And even more perplexing to Josephine, each staff member had recently been issued with the newest model iPhone. In her opinion, productivity in the company was limited enough without providing extra gadgets, and unnecessarily extravagant gadgets, to distract staff even further.

After picking up a cardigan somebody had carelessly dropped onto the floor, Josephine wheeled the trolley into the alcove where the senior staff sat. Donna, one of the longest serving secretaries, and also one of the nastiest, was the only person there.

'I hope that's skim milk,' she said rudely as Josephine set down her cup and saucer.

'Same as every other day Donna,' Josephine replied, amazed that somebody who smoked a pack a day was so concerned about her health.

After finishing the morning tea run, Josephine retraced her steps to collect all the cups and plates. She wondered why it was that people had to leave that last little piece of biscuit or cake on their plates and dregs of tea and coffee in their cups, but she gathered them up without complaint and went back to her workspace to wash up and make preparations for the afternoon tea run.

Despite the wealth of the company, Blackstone paid little attention to the needs of the tea lady. Josephine's workspace was a tiny recess off the kitchen with a small sink. There was no dishwasher and you couldn't swing a cat in the small space. Yet the cups and plates were always scrupulously clean and the cutlery sparkled. Previously, her job had been done by two people, yet she managed it easily alone, something of which she was very proud. She could not be faulted on her work. There was no wastage and expenditure for morning and afternoon teas had remained unchanged for two years due to her careful budgeting.

At lunchtime Josephine went for a walk to stretch her legs and then sat in the Botanical Gardens to eat her sandwiches. She never ate in the staff room. She knew none of the other women in the office liked her and besides she found their conversations about shopping and socialising tedious. In the ten years Josephine had worked at Blackstone she could remember buying her lunch only twice. She simply couldn't fathom paying more for a single sandwich than for an entire loaf of bread at the supermarket. Day old bread was even cheaper and you could hardly notice the difference.

After completing the afternoon tea round, cleaning up and organising things for the next day, another work day was over for Josephine. She buttoned her jacket, collected her handbag and set off for the train station. The trip home was slightly quicker, given that she finished earlier than most city office workers. Upon arriving home before 5.15 pm every day, she would follow an unvarying routine each night.

Dinner was at 6.30 pm. She bought her supplies in bulk at a discount wholesaler and on the first Saturday of each month she would cook up a month's supply of meals to go in the freezer. Take-away was never a temptation. After finishing her meal and washing up, Josephine watched an hour of television on the portable set she had purchased at a garage sale for fifteen dollars. Sure the colour was a bit wonky and there was no remote control, but she was used to it now. What did it matter if everything on the screen was tinged in green anyway?

Switching off the TV at 8.30 pm, Josephine settled back in her armchair for an hour of reading. The armchair was also a garage sale purchase. She loved to read. A member of two libraries, each fortnight she would select five new titles. She didn't believe in buying books for herself.

Every night before climbing into bed Josephine would look around at her little home with pride. In exchange for caretaking a large house, while the owners travelled frequently, she was allowed to live in the detached ground floor flat rent-free. She had to pay her own utilities and food, but that was minimal enough. After living there for almost two decades she considered it to be her home and had no desire to move anywhere else.

• • • • •

One Friday morning a month later, Jerry was bleary eyed on the train. After partying until the early hours he had only managed two hours sleep and wasn't sure he could face a morning making egg sandwiches. As far as hangovers went, this was a decent one. He opted out of the card game, concentrating instead on sitting perfectly still and not thinking about food.

The seat next to Josephine promised to be a safe bet. She would not expect him to make conversation nor would she lecture him about his self-inflicted discomfort. So preoccupied with his nausea, Jerry didn't notice Josephine studying the business pages of the paper with great interest.

Nor did he notice Amanda's desperate attempts to get his attention. As Josephine was so engrossed in the paper she hadn't noticed her handbag had fallen open on the seat next to her. Amanda couldn't believe that Jerry was wasting such a great opportunity to snoop on Sister Josephine, or whoever she was. They had been waiting years for a chance like this! After biting viciously into an apple she tried some mental telepathy. That didn't work either. It would be far too pointed to peer into the bag herself, although she did briefly consider it.

As they got off the train, Amanda caught up to Jerry but her glare went unnoticed because as soon as they cleared the doorway he started running towards the nearest toilets. Throwing her apple core at Jerry's fleeing form Amanda headed for the escalators, typing an abusive text message to him as she walked. Jerry, however, was too busy throwing up to hear the beep as the message came through.

Before she even entered the building Josephine knew things would be tense. And she was right. There were no clusters of people gossiping in the foyer and management spent the entire morning huddled together in David Green's office. Josephine served them tea and coffee as they talked in anxious tones.

Rumours of problems within the company had been circulating for months, but the staff all believed it was merely speculation. Today's newspaper article had brought the dire reality to everybody's attention, sending a wave of panic around the office.

Josephine was washing up when one of the junior secretaries delivered the memo. Addressed to all staff the message was printed on plain paper instead of the usual heavy, embossed stock the company favoured. Wiping her hands on a hand towel, Josephine paused to slip her glasses on before reading:

While media speculation is, as usual, sensationalised and exaggerated, it is true that Blackstone is experiencing some moderate cash flow problems. We have been instructed to prepare a report for the auditors to be presented at a Board Meeting in two weeks' time. Until then we ask that all staff be prudent in their use of company resources and mindful of productivity levels. To facilitate this, the following changes will take effect immediately:

- *All long distance calls must be cleared through the switch.*
- *There will be no paid overtime or meal allowances under any circumstances.*
- *The employee subsidy at Fi Fi's Café is hereby cancelled.*

We trust that you will all work with us to ensure our company's future.

David Green,
Managing Director

As Josephine carefully folded the memo and put it in her bag, she couldn't help but smile.

• • • • •

The change in atmosphere around the office was

immediate and noticeable. All the staff seemed to be outdoing themselves in an effort to make their positions indispensable. Josephine had never seen the young secretaries work so hard. When she heard Bella sobbing in the toilets about how she needed her job to pay for her upcoming wedding, Josephine wondered if it was inhuman to have little sympathy for a person who had contributed to her own downfall. Bella's reputation for spending the majority of her workday making personal phone calls and surfing the internet was right on the money.

Gerald Pitts gave Josephine his usual look of contempt as she brought in his afternoon tea one day. 'You'd better make the most of your job while it lasts Josie,' he sneered, 'tea ladies are generally the first to go.'

Josephine shrugged. 'Anything is possible in this world Mr Pitts. You know what they say about life's upheavals often being blessings in disguise.'

'I'm sure there are plenty of award wage servant's jobs out there,' Gerald said. 'I suggest you start looking very soon.'

In response, Josephine offered a cold, insincere smile that unnerved Gerald more than he cared to admit.

Blackstone's financial woes were soon well known in the business community. It was a source of gossip in many other companies and there were varying opinions about what was behind their downfall. Having recently retired from Blackstone, Kevin Jeffries followed the story with great interest and a week after the announcement he and some friends dissected the situation over a long lunch at his riverside mansion.

'Overstaffing is the biggest problem,' he said as he lit his customary post-meal cigar. 'Too many chiefs and far too many Indians. There's too many perks for the younger ones too. Why should some kid in the mail room have a company funded mobile phone?'

Gerald Pitts nodded glumly and pointedly moved his chair out of the path of Kevin's cigar smoke. It was easy for Kevin to say that now, with his golden handshake cheque cashed. Gerald knew that his former colleague had ridden the gravy boat in style for many years and had reaped countless rewards from it. At least five years from retirement, Gerald was feeling decidedly nervous about his future with Blackstone.

After its two week stay of execution the moment of truth arrived for Blackstone when the auditors moved in. After the board meeting and presentation of the audit report, a specialised management committee was sent in. This was not seen as a positive sign for Blackstone's future. All media reports also suggested it was not looking good for the former blue-chip company.

So the news that the company would trade on was unexpected but very welcome. Staff were warned, however, to brace themselves for some savage cost cutting to ride out the storm.

Unsurprisingly the first fall of the axe was on staffing levels, resulting in a wave of retrenchments. One by one, each employee was called into the boardroom to meet with the

Management Committee. Those lucky enough to retain their jobs were informed of their new reduced salary packages and loss of fringe benefits. The rest were asked to leave the building within the hour.

As Josephine was required to keep the coffee cups of the Management Committee topped up, she was privy to the downfall of Blackstone's former high flyers. Most took the news stoically, but the atmosphere in the room was more oppressive than anything she had ever experienced. Although her face remained impassive the entire time, Josephine was particularly satisfied to see Gerald and Frank being handed their pink slips.

The bloodletting lasted almost three hours. The upshot was that Blackstone had been relieved of nine senior managers, eight secretaries and twelve administration staff. A security guard escorted each of the retrenched staff members out of the building after they had packed their belongings and said their goodbyes.

The Management Committee remained in the building for the rest of the day, completing their paperwork and making the necessary arrangements for the company to continue in its new, leaner form. At four o'clock, the head of the committee Simon Nelson asked senior secretary Donna to summon Josephine to the boardroom.

Donna smirked as she made her way to the kitchen recess. Smugly comfortable about keeping her job, she was looking forward to witnessing Josephine's almost certain downfall. And she wasn't the only one. The staff who remained had been watching all day for the tea lady to be called to the boardroom.

Josephine noticed Donna's self-satisfied look but said nothing as she made her way to the boardroom.

'Sit down,' Simon said with a tired smile, as Josephine hovered politely near the door. Removing his glasses for a moment, Simon rubbed his eyes. What a day! Despite what many people believed, he never enjoyed the task of telling people that they had been fired.

Josephine sat and waited expectantly.

'Well, did that go as you wanted it to?' he asked.

In all the years Simon had worked in his current position he had never come across a set of circumstances quite like this. Sure, it wasn't unheard of for an anonymous investor to come forward and rescue a company that had gone belly up due to its own mismanagement, and there had even been occasions when the investor had been an employee of the company. But never before had he sat down with the tea lady, who was considered to occupy the lowest position on the professional totem pole, and discussed how her money had saved the company.

They talked business for half an hour, sorting out paperwork and other formalities. Then, as Josephine rose to leave the room a thoughtful expression crossed her face. 'I've been rethinking the secretaries,' she said. 'I think we can afford to lose another one. I'll tell Donna to come back in and see you now.'

Simon nodded but kept his expression neutral. Blackstone had no idea what was in store for them with Josephine at the helm.

Josephine rode the train home as always, although today she couldn't help but feel a small sense of satisfaction. She knew that Simon and the others had been dying to ask how on earth she had managed to do it, but they had refrained. She had to give them points for restraint.

There was no danger that Simon would have caught Josephine in a weak moment and found out her story. Josephine had vowed that nobody would ever know of her impoverished childhood, nor of her first job at fourteen working as a toilet cleaner in a shopping centre. The years spent watching her father throw every last cent away at the local TAB and her mother passively accepting it rather than getting a job herself had borne in Josephine a fierce determination for financial security.

On her first day of work she had promised herself that she would never squander her hard earned money and she had lived up to that. It had not been as difficult as many would imagine. In fact Josephine's financial strategy was quite simple – to put away more than she spent each week, to choose a conservative investment strategy and to never, ever be impulsive in her spending.

Upon arriving home, Josephine followed her normal nightly routine and was in bed by 9.30 pm. She wondered how the day ahead would pan out. Her intention was to remain in her position as tea lady and to not reveal her identity to anybody outside the Management Committee. Simon would probably have been surprised to know that as well as her majority share in Blackstone, she was also a major investor in two other companies and had an extensive property portfolio.

Funnily enough she had read an article about millionaires in *Woman's Day* on her way home that afternoon. The lifestyles described bore no resemblance to hers, but she was used to that. Josephine assumed her name was on a list somewhere but nobody had ever come and asked her about her life. She supposed that a millionaire who lived in a small unit on somebody else's property and who slept in a twenty-year-old single bed and had an old-fashioned alarm clock, was not that exciting.

But Josephine didn't care. All that mattered to her was that she had lived up to her own promises and that she knew for certain her financial future was secure.

• • • • •

Grace was surprised by how much she had enjoyed reading the first story and even wished it had been longer. She had only used fifteen minutes of her hour so far. Turning the page over she prepared to start on the next one but then remembered what Sylvia had said. 'Um, would you like me to talk about the story?' she asked, glancing at Edith.

The blink again and a lopsided smile.

Grace looked down at the text again and considered her answer. 'Well, I thought Josephine was kind of misunderstood.'

Another blink from Edith.

Grace took this as her cue to continue. 'I think all everybody saw was what was on the surface, someone who was plain and boring and old fashioned. But underneath she was actually really smart and determined.'

Grace shuffled her position to avoid the jutting spring at the back of the recliner, and wondered why Edith kept the decrepit old chair. Then again, no doubt it was the kind of chair Josephine would keep and use. Perhaps Edith shared some characteristics with Josephine? Or had in her former life.

Thinking for a moment she framed her next comments as best she could to avoid any offence about old people and things. 'Um, on the whole Josephine is very rigid and literally didn't seem to care what people thought of her. But that can be a good quality sometimes. No matter what most people say they DO care what other people think of them. To be like Josephine and really not care is pretty rare.'

Two blinks this time. Grace assumed that meant Edith really agreed with her. Encouraged she continued on. 'I really liked the twist at the end. I was so wrapped up in the other elements of the story I didn't see it coming at all. I liked how she got back at the mean guys in her own quiet way.'

A definite smile this time.

'Yeah,' Grace added softly. 'It's a shame not everybody has the guts to do that.'

Talking about the other elements of the story helped the time pass quickly and when the hour ticked over and she knew she could go Grace wasn't quite as excited to leave as she had anticipated earlier. Slipping the book back in the cluttered drawer she stood up, resisting the urge to rub her aching lower back. 'Well, if that's all I guess I'll be going now…'

Edith blinked and smiled.

'All right, see you,' Grace said, backing towards the door. Giving an awkward little wave she opened the door and inched out into the hallway.

As she drove home Grace felt strangely exhilarated. She had endured the humiliation of talking about her personal circumstances without having a panic attack. And she had made conversation with a stranger without feeling horrifically self-conscious. On her way there, she'd gotten herself so worked up about what she would have to do but it had been nowhere near as bad as she had feared. Perhaps her counsellor Melanie was right in that she spent too much time thinking and over-analysing and not enough time just doing.

But then again if she didn't think and analyse then she couldn't keep a handle on things. And keeping a handle on things was the key to everything. Take today for example. If she hadn't thought ahead she wouldn't have known to take the detour on the back streets instead of the freeway. Sure it took longer and there were dozens of sets of traffic lights to sit through but that was okay. Anything was better than driving past *that* place.

Oh no, why had she dared to even think of it? That was the whole purpose of physically avoiding it, now even thinking about not thinking about it was enough to set her off.

Glancing out the window at the school pick up traffic that was starting to build, Grace knew she had to get a grip on herself. 'Breath Grace, breathe', she chanted softly, glad she was stopped at a red light and had a moment to pull herself together. 'You can make it home,' she reassured herself.

White knuckling the steering wheel she focused on the traffic light. The second it turned green she planted her foot, desperate to leave the unsettling thoughts at the intersection and make it to the safety of home.

* * * * *

She had loved driving before.

While other people from small towns were often nervous in the traffic and fretted about getting lost in the hustle and bustle of Brisbane's congested roads, Grace embraced the challenge. Of course it was all the more fun in a brand new car, lovingly bestowed upon her by doting parents the day she left her home town for the bright lights of the city. She couldn't believe they had impulsively cashed in a long held insurance policy to buy it for her, especially when they drove a twenty-year-old Commodore themselves. But she had loved the little Peugeot upon sight and had relished every single moment of that maiden voyage.

Everybody had warned her about the traffic lights before she left. Coming from a place where there were none within a one hundred kilometre radius, they were viewed with suspicion at the very least but mostly with contempt. 'Fancy having to sit still on an empty road just because some robotic light tells you to,' her elderly neighbour Mr Fargus had declared with a fearful shake of his head. 'If city people had even a quarter of the manners we have out here you wouldn't need the blasted things.'

Her mother was more concerned about her personal safety. 'Only look straight ahead Gracie,' she advised, worry etched into her face. 'Otherwise those road ragers will come after you.'

Grace had taken the advice sagely, but in truth she loved the traffic lights. To her they represented the essence of city life and the fact that you were surrounded by enough people to need a way to keep some kind of order. In fact, she deliberately drove on the surface streets most of the time so she could feel the rhythm of the traffic. Rhythm had always been at the core of her being.

Well it used to be anyway.

Although she wasn't anywhere near as panicky as she had been on her first visit, Grace was still a bundle of nerves when she arrived at Rosehill Gardens the following week. She hadn't thought to ask if she needed to check in with Sylvia each week or if there was a form she needed to get signed to give her case worker. And what if she was stopped in the hallway and asked who she was and why she was there?

As it happened the receptionist glanced up as she walked in. 'Hello,' she said pleasantly. 'The visitors register is just around the corner on the white table.'

'Right, thank you,' Grace replied. Problem solved without any drama.

Navigating her way down to Edith's room, she avoided meeting the eyes of any of the other residents she met along the way. She wasn't ready for any other interactions at this place just yet and besides it seemed most of them were too focused on their own issues to worry about her.

All except the gnome like man with eyes the colour of a summer sky. 'Cheer up love, it might never happen,' he said with an impish grin as he whizzed past in an electric wheelchair.

Grace paused for a second trying to think up an appropriate reply. But the man was long gone. People were always telling her she looked too serious, but how else were you supposed to look when your life was a mess? She watched his fleeing form for a few seconds, the memory of those bright blue eyes fixed in her mind. She had always assumed that your eyes dulled as you got older, but clearly they didn't, well maybe unless you had cataracts or something.

Grace shook her head and kept walking, pausing when she got to room 46. It had been easier last time when Sylvia had announced her arrival. A wave of uncertainty hit. Was she allowed to just go in herself? Should she have asked someone to escort her? Maybe I should knock first, she decided. She'd gotten as far as lifting her hand when she realised the futility of her action. How was a woman who couldn't speak going to respond to a knock? Idiot, she thought.

Steeling herself she grabbed the handle and opened the door before she could dither any further.

Once again Edith was dressed in a bright bed jacket and her hair was beautifully styled. An elegant woman wearing a beautician's uniform was sitting beside the bed finishing a French manicure. Noticing Grace she smiled. 'Hello I'm Dominique.'

'Grace,' she murmured in reply, her expression unable to hide the surprise she felt at the scene before her.

'Just because Edith doesn't use her hands much doesn't mean they shouldn't look nice,' Dominique said. 'It's amazing how a manicure can give you a lift.'

Grace shook her head as her face glowed red. 'Oh, I'm so sorry! I didn't mean to stare, it's just that I have never got the whole nail thing and I just didn't realise that in here you would be able to do that kind of thing...'

Dominique laughed. 'Of course you can, it's not a prison.'

'No, no, of course not. I just meant I didn't know people came in to do that.'

'I've done Edith's nails for years and I told her I'd keep

doing them as long as she wants me to.'

'That's great. Gosh mine are just embarrassing,' Grace said, clenching her hands into fists to hide the offending nails from sight.

'Well it's never too late to get them into shape,' Dominique said as she packed up her gear. 'We have a half price special every Wednesday. I'm at Gloria's Beauty Bar in the city.'

Grace nodded. 'Thanks, I'll remember that,' she said, knowing that at even at half price she could not afford a manicure or any other kind of beauty treatment.

'All done Edith,' Dominique said brightly, taking the time to arrange the frail woman's hands carefully on the top of her bedclothes. 'No housework today, you hear?'

Edith smiled and blinked as Dominique lifted her bag and prepared to leave.

Grace smiled too, amazed that the other woman dared to joke about Edith's condition. Wasn't that offensive? But no, Edith had smiled in response so maybe not.

She stepped back as Dominique stood, intimidated by her perfect makeup and impeccable dress.

'See you in a fortnight Gorgeous,' Dominique said, leaning down to kiss Edith on the cheek. 'Nice to meet you Grace,' she said as she walked towards the door. 'Come in anytime for that manicure.'

'Yeah, sure,' Grace murmured, trying to sound sincere. Taking a deep breath she sat down and picked up the book that was sitting ready on the bedside table.

Adrenaline surged as Sarah Harris explained the final details of the wedding photography package she was selling, but she maintained perfect composure. She had learned early on to always remain calm and professional with her clients, even when large sums of money were being discussed.

Vanessa Morrison flipped through the sample album for the most expensive package, her shell pink fingernails tapping lightly on each page as she examined the layouts. Meanwhile, Sarah discreetly studied the woman sitting on the couch opposite. Her navy blue Carla Zampatti suit was wrinkle free, her makeup flawless and not a strand of glossy auburn hair was out of place. Sarah had seen Vanessa arriving in a silver Mercedes coupe, a car that seemed to fit in perfectly with the shiny, upscale life she obviously lived.

Over the past four years Sarah had worked very hard to attract clients just like Vanessa. She had started her photography career in a large studio but had soon grown impatient with people who haggled over the cost of each shot and took years to pay off their family portraits. Careful research had shown that wedding photography was where the big money was and, more importantly, that well off brides-to-be were the ones that paid their way with interest. So, that was the niche market she had aggressively pursued.

Sarah could tell if she wanted a potential client the moment they walked into her studio. The young women who looked around in awe and seemed nervous were regretfully informed that their date was already booked. On the other hand, those who were nonchalant in the luxurious studio surroundings were given red carpet treatment.

Although the expensive office space Sarah leased had kept her business running at a loss for the first year, the investment had paid off. These days all her clients were of the highest calibre, which was reflected in the ongoing increase in her income.

Vanessa closed the album and pushed it back towards the centre of the table. 'That's exactly what we've been looking for,' she said with a smile. 'I'll take this one and we'll happily pay the surcharge to have them done as a priority.'

Careful not to display any emotion, Sarah nodded. 'Lovely. I'll get a contract drawn up and have it out to you by next week.'

• • • • •

Over the following months Vanessa continued to be a model customer, following Sarah's advice without question and making the necessary decisions without drama. At her last appointment a week before the wedding, Sarah was amazed at her calm and unruffled state. This was not unusual in Sarah's experience of wealthy families though. More often than not there was a wedding planner employed to take all the stress as last minute problems cropped up and the bride would have little else to do but partake in beauty treatments and drink champagne.

'You wouldn't believe how excited my parents are,' Vanessa said as she read through the timetable Sarah had drawn up for the big day. 'Dad is insisting on paying for everything, although Marcus and I would happily chip in.'

Sarah nodded and smiled. 'Oh well, if he wants to pay let him pay. I think most fathers like to give their daughters the best wedding possible.'

After she had wished Vanessa luck for the coming week and waved her off, Sarah started packing up for the day. Preparing her banking, she couldn't help but smile at the total on the bottom of the deposit slip. Rich people didn't quibble about the cost and more often than not Daddy was picking up the tab, so the bride didn't even look at the quote, or question the extra charges she always managed to sneak in at the last minute.

• • • • •

As she headed west the following Saturday Sarah squinted in the morning sun. Wriggling her toes, she scanned the road for the unmarked turn off. It must be along here somewhere. Sarah's accelerator foot was starting to cramp after almost two hours of driving and she was well and truly bored with the passing scenery.

Finally a crooked tree with a reflective arrow on it came into view. 'About bloody time!' Sarah exclaimed. Slowing, she made the turn onto a narrow, winding road with only a thin strip of bitumen in its centre. Two kilometres along she came across an old drum that had been converted into a letterbox. Turning again Sarah cringed as her Corolla bounced into a large pothole. She wondered if the car's suspension would survive the trip along the unsealed driveway surface. Slowing to a crawl, Sarah hoped her equipment had not been damaged. How does Vanessa's Mercedes survive this goat track? she wondered.

When the house finally came into view Sarah was floored. Working among an almost exclusively wealthy clientele she was used to arriving at large, prestigious homes. Some were genuine mansions. She soaked up such experiences, ever careful not to act impressed. A simple comment along the lines of, 'a lovely place you have here', was as far as she ever went.

When Vanessa mentioned she was getting ready for her wedding at her parents rural property outside Toowoomba, Sarah knew it would be one of the grandest homes in the area. She wasn't expecting a sandstone mansion with large pillars at the front – in her mind it was more likely to be a beautifully restored Queenslander with landscaped grounds. There would definitely be a pool and probably a tennis court as well, given that they had lots of land.

Dumfounded at the sight before her, Sarah realised she must have taken a wrong turn somewhere. The decrepit farmhouse at the end of the driveway could not possibly be Vanessa's family home. Not when there were two treads missing off the front stairs, the last paint job had obviously been done several decades before and the guttering was hanging precariously, attached only by rusty wire.

Damn it, she thought crossly. I'll have to go back to the turn off. Turning the ignition back on, Sarah drove forward so she could turn around. It was only then that she saw Vanessa's Mercedes parked in between two rusted out car bodies.

For a moment Sarah sat in her car, trying to process this new turn of events. How had her filtering system failed so badly? Maybe I could just sneak away, she thought wildly. I'll call and say I'm hopelessly lost and will never make it in time.

But then her practical side took over. Vanessa had already paid a fifty per cent deposit on the most expensive package, with the balance due in two weeks. It would be stupid to pass up that kind of money.

The moment she stepped out of her car, two large Dobermans lunged at her from nowhere, barking loudly. Not a dog lover, Sarah cowered in fright. Pressed up against the driver's door, she was too scared to even register the muddy footprints they had splattered on her new black skirt.

Fortunately a booming voice yelled, 'Oscar! Ernie! Down!'

Although this voice had little impact on the dogs' behaviour, at least it meant that somebody could see her and might rescue her before she was mauled. Sarah almost cried in relief when a man appeared and shooed the beasts away. Dressed in ragged shorts, a faded flannelette shirt, gumboots and a straw hat, his face was partially hidden behind a bushy grey beard.

'G'day love, you must be the photographer. I'm Len, the father of the bride,' he announced proudly thrusting a dirty, calloused hand towards her.

Still shaken Sarah could only nod and give a weak smile as she reluctantly returned Len's enthusiastic handshake. 'Sarah Harris.'

'Sorry about the dogs. They're a bit rowdy sometimes, wouldn't hurt a fly though.'

Sarah gave another lukewarm smile. People always said that *their* dog would never hurt a fly, but she begged to differ. She had been scared too many times by dogs that barked ferociously and bared their teeth menacingly, to believe that all dogs were harmless. Still, she was out of harm's way for now.

Unlocking the boot, Sarah started unpacking her equipment. About to stack it on the ground, she was pleasantly surprised when Len appeared behind her with outstretched arms and said, 'Load me up love, you shouldn't have to carry all that heavy gear inside yourself.'

Apparently chivalry was not dead after all.

As she followed Len around the side of the house to the back door Sarah did a quick rethink of the situation. Maybe Vanessa's family had pressured her to get ready at home? Yes, that was probably it. She had said that her father had insisted on paying for everything, but obviously that didn't extend to springing for a nice hotel room somewhere. Vanessa must be mortified about me coming here, Sarah thought sympathetically.

Len led her though a ramshackle kitchen with dirty plates on every surface into a large, untidy lounge room. Sitting on a lumpy couch with a torn cover was Vanessa and her two bridesmaids. Their hair and makeup was done and they were painting their nails. A woman in a faded blue chenille dressing gown and bare feet sat on a wooden kitchen chair, drinking a cup of tea, looking every inch the country hick.

'Oh, hi Sarah,' Vanessa said. 'You found the place okay?'

'Yes, no problems,' Sarah replied briskly, still thrown by her surroundings.

'This is my mum Valerie,' Vanessa said, pointing to the woman in the dressing gown, 'and these are my sisters Bridget and Fran.'

Vanessa made the introductions with a radiant smile and offered no excuses for the state of the house. To Sarah's amazement she didn't seem embarrassed at all.

Valerie smiled warmly. 'Would you like a cuppa love?'

Sarah shook her head. She was dying for a coffee, but there was no way she was touching anything from that kitchen.

Sarah looked long and hard at the lounge room while everybody got dressed, attempting to find the least objectionable background she could. Alone in the shabby room, she could only shake her head at what she had to contend with. Half of one wall was taken up with an old-fashioned china cabinet. Walking over closer Sarah discovered some nice pieces of china inside. It was just a shame that a large souvenir teaspoon collection dominated the top three shelves, overshadowing everything else. She simply didn't understand the philosophy of collecting spoons and displaying them in a plastic case. There were spoons from Darwin, Oodnadatta, Broome, Hobart and dozens of places in between and each was as gaudy as the next. Scratch that wall, Sarah thought crossly.

Len entered the lounge room, a pair of black lace-up shoes in his hand. 'Great collection hey?' he said proudly.

Sarah gave one of her best fake smiles and nodded in response.

'Started it up when I was just a nipper and since then people just know to get me a spoon whenever they go somewhere. I've never travelled much myself, never been much further than Brisbane actually, but these spoons here they make me feel a bit more worldly, know what I mean?'

Sarah nodded in a way she hoped didn't seem insincere.

'If I get a second before we leave I'll tell you some good stories about how I came across some of them. But I've been ordered to clean my shoes first.'

When Len left the room Sarah studied the next wall. It was covered haphazardly with dozens of family photographs – baby photos, school shots, family portraits and various others – all housed in cheap frames and many of the photos had begun to stick to the glass. Scratch that wall as well.

The next area she looked at housed a television circa 1980 in a wooden cabinet, a dusty VCR and a record player that sat atop several shelves of records. Two large speakers were perched precariously on mismatched wooden tables on either side of the TV. So that area was no good either.

Beginning to get desperate Sarah glanced over to the entrance of the hallway. Fortunately there was one bare patch of wall painted a cacky yellow colour, which would just have to do. Thanks to Photoshop she would be able to doctor the background later.

As the day wore on Sarah worked hard to quell her frustration. Keeping up a façade of enthusiasm and interest in proceedings was taking a lot of effort. Only the thought of the final payment kept her going. Quite frankly, she didn't even want to be seen in public with these people, let alone photograph them.

More than anything Sarah was angry with Vanessa for misleading her. At the very least the bride could have pulled her aside and apologised for having such a hillbilly family, yet she was acting like the entire thing was completely acceptable. There hadn't been so much as an eye roll or an exasperated sigh from the Vanessa while Len tramped around telling coarse jokes and Valerie boasted that she had won a perm for the big day via a raffle at the pub.

Sarah couldn't understand where Vanessa got her confidence from. In Sarah's view of the world people who grew up in the backblocks in rackety old houses had to earn their way to the top. And, if by some small chance they made it, then they should work hard to hide their background, not flaunt it. Who did Vanessa think she was driving a silver Mercedes when she had grown up in squalor?

Squinting into the lens of the camera, Sarah tried to line up a respectable family shot. Despite everything, Vanessa looked beautiful, so why hadn't she insisted that her father trim his beard or better still shave it off? Why was she letting him wear a suit that was at least two decades old and a size too small? And would it have killed Vanessa to buy her mother a nice dress for the day instead of letting her show up in what could best be described as a house dress? Sarah knew her photography skills could not be shown to their best advantage when she had so little to work with.

'All right, chins up everybody, shoulders out and smile,' Sarah instructed with all the enthusiasm she could muster. After taking the shot Sarah studied the image on the digital screen. Len had his eyes closed, again.

Sarah took a deep breath. 'Okay let's have one more, everybody eyes open wide please.'

When Vanessa had issued Sarah an invitation to the wedding dinner, she had eagerly accepted. She always enjoyed rubbing shoulders with an upper class social set. However once she had lay eyes on the house that morning, Sarah had hatched a plan to feign a headache and escape as fast as possible.

By the time the bridal party arrived at the reception venue, however, Sarah had changed her mind again. A free meal was a free meal and she knew if she didn't ingest something alcoholic very soon she might just lose the plot. Besides her feet were killing her as the straps of her new sandals now felt like they were made of barbed wire.

After stowing her equipment carefully in her car, Sarah was led to an empty space at the end of one of the outer tables. The glass of champagne she'd skulled on arrival had taken the edge off her bad temper and she was actually able to rustle up a smile.

'Welcome to the misfit's end of the table,' slurred a middle-aged man with a red face. 'I'm Uncle Arthur and I like my booze so I'm always exiled to the back corner at these events.'

Sarah nodded and gave an almost genuine sympathetic smile. 'Well the photographer always gets stuck in the corner as well so you can tell me all the family secrets.'

By the time the dessert plates were cleared away, Uncle Arthur had not drawn a breath. Fuelled by numerous vodka tonics he really *had* shared all the family secrets, as boring as they had turned out to be. Sarah, who had enjoyed a few champagnes herself, was at the point where she could nod about every thirty seconds without really having to listen. I really should get going, she thought, but I'm still probably a bit over the limit.

'I'm surprised Valerie didn't wear the family jewels,' Uncle Arthur slurred. 'What better place to wear them than a family wedding?'

'Mmmm,' agreed Sarah absently, examining her ragged pinkie nail. She always bit her nails when she was frustrated and the pinkie had taken a real battering today.

Uncle Arthur took another swallow of his drink. 'You know some people think rubies are old fashioned, but I reckon they're pretty classy.'

With that he caught Sarah's attention for the first time in almost an hour. Gulping down a glass of water in an attempt to clear her head she turned to Uncle Arthur and flashed him a radiant smile. 'Sorry what did you say?'

'Well my prostate problems started about five years ago,' he began, taking another slug of vodka.

'No, no, the thing about the family jewels.'

'Oh, that,' he replied. 'Well Lenny's mother left him a ruby necklace that's about a hundred years old. Worth a packet, but he won't sell it. Reckons his great grandmother would haunt him if he did. Valerie won't wear it – she's not the type – and because he's got three daughters he can't give it to one of them without offending the others.'

Sarah gulped down another glass of water. 'So, he just has it sitting in a bank vault or something?'

'Bank vault?' Arthur snorted. 'Are you kidding? Lenny hates banks. Nah he's got it in a glass case sitting in his shed. Tells people it's just a fake, but a few family members know the real story.' Arthur tapped his nose conspiratorially.

'Oh yes, mum's the word,' Sarah agreed. 'Can I get you another drink?'

'Sure honey, but just make it a small one.'

'Righto,' Sarah said, heading off to the bar.

It didn't take long for Uncle Arthur to pass out after Sarah presented him with a triple strength vodka. Gulping down her strong, black coffee, Sarah made the most of the opportunity to depart, leaving Uncle Arthur snoring on the tabletop.

Speeding along the quiet road two hours later, Sarah barely registered the speedometer nudging one hundred and twenty kilometres per hour. Aware that she was still probably over the limit, she could only hope that there were no RBT teams out and about. Glancing at the fuel gauge Sarah did a double take. It had been half full when she arrived at the reception and now it was down to a quarter.

'Stupid car,' she yelled, banging her hand on the steering wheel. 'Where am I going to get petrol out here?' She cast her mind back to the journey that morning and tried to remember where she had seen a servo and decided to keep driving and hope for the best, almost certain there had been one not too far back from the turn off.

Finally the lights of a service station came into view. Breathing a sigh of relief, Sarah braked sharply and turned into the driveway, not bothering to use her indicator. There wasn't much point when there wasn't another car on the road in either direction.

Sarah yawned as she filled her tank. It was almost 12.15 am and the thought of the long drive home to Brisbane was depressing. I've got a good mind to tack my fuel costs on to Vanessa's final bill she thought crossly, especially since petrol is twelve cents a litre more expensive out here. Shivering in the cool night air Sarah briefly considered her personal safety as another car pulled into the driveway. Being attacked in the middle of nowhere was all she needed right now.

Trying not to be obvious about it she glanced over at the thirty-something man who had just pulled up at bowser two. Dressed in faded jeans and a Hard Yakka work shirt, he appeared harmless enough and completely disinterested in what she was doing. Still Sarah was relieved when the pump clicked to indicate her tank was full and she could head for the relative safety of the shop.

The attendant was sorting a pile of receipts and seemed pleased to have a chance to make conversation.

'Rough day?' he asked pleasantly, eyeing the king sized Mars bar and two litre bottle of Coke Sarah plonked on the counter.

'Don't even start with me,' Sarah growled, her reserves of politeness well and truly exhausted.

The young man dropped his gaze, his demeanour changing in response to Sarah's rude reply. 'Whatever. That's forty-three dollars sixty with the fuel.'

'Here keep the change,' Sarah snapped, throwing a fifty dollar bill on the counter and stomping outside.

Sarah sat in her car for a minute devouring the chocolate bar with little enjoyment. Taking a swig of soft drink straight from the bottle, she cursed Uncle Arthur and his drunken stories. Her trip out to the Morrison's place had been a complete waste of time. There had been no ruby necklace in the shed. Despite her extensive search she had found no precious jewels whatsoever. If that wasn't bad enough, her hands would be grease stained for weeks after pawing through piles of engine parts and she had broken the heel off one of her designer shoes. The roll of fifty dollar notes she had pocketed were little in the way of compensation, in fact, she felt she had earned them fair and square that day.

• • • • •

Buoyed by the anticipation of Vanessa's final payment, Sarah managed to get over her annoyance at what a debacle the whole thing had ended up being. It's almost kind of funny, she thought as she slid Vanessa and Marcus' album into its velvet-lined box two weeks later, but I'll have to make sure it doesn't happen again. I'm not re-living a day like that, no matter how good the financial reward.

As arranged Vanessa arrived promptly at four o'clock. Sarah couldn't help but stare at the other woman as she walked through the door. With her hair in a ponytail and no makeup she looked about sixteen. And she was wearing unflattering navy trousers and a pale blue fleece jumper. What was she thinking when she dressed today?

Now if she'd showed up at the first appointment looking like that, this whole thing never would have happened, Sarah thought wryly. Switching to professional mode, she showed her client to the main office.

'So nice to see you again Vanessa,' she said politely. 'Your album is all done as per instructions and it looks magnificent if I do say so myself.'

'Great,' Vanessa replied. 'I can't wait to see it.'

'Well, I can show you now if you like.'

'Uh, no, thanks I really can't stay long,' Vanessa replied. 'I'll give you a call after I've had a look at it.'

'Sure whatever suits you. I'll just get your invoice,' Sarah said, flipping through a folder on the counter. 'Okay, here we go. As discussed, the final payment is due today.'

'No problem,' Vanessa replied, accepting the bill and scanning it. Reaching into her handbag she pulled out a chequebook. 'Can I borrow a pen?'

Sarah handed her a blue Kilometrico and Vanessa quickly filled in a cheque and handed it over.

'Thanks,' said Sarah, unable to stop the smile that

always accompanied receipt of a payment. Studying the cheque for a moment she frowned slightly. 'Uh Vanessa, you've made an error here,' she pointed out. This amount is four hundred dollars short.'

Vanessa didn't blink. 'Oh no, I'm just taking into account the money you stole from my father.'

'I beg your pardon?' Sarah's heart leapt to her throat.

'Oh, I think you know exactly what I mean.'

At that moment the door pinged as someone walked into the outer office. Flustered, Sarah looked towards the other room then back at Vanessa.

'Answer the door,' Vanessa said. 'I'm not going anywhere.'

'Really, you're mistaken,' Sarah stammered. 'I'll just send this person away and we can sort this out.'

In the outer office she received her second shock of the day. '*Uncle Arthur?*'

'That's Detective Arthur actually,' he said, flipping open a wallet and showing his badge.

'What the…?' Sarah exclaimed, struggling to maintain her professional demeanour. Then Vanessa emerged, unzipping her fleece as she walked across the room to reveal a police uniform.

'Oh shit,' Sarah murmured, sinking down onto the plush couch and burying her head in her hands.

Sarah was surprised by the speed of the whole arrest process. The reading of her rights, handcuffing and transport to the police station where she was fingerprinted and questioned, all occurred with the efficiency of a well-oiled machine. Supporting Uncle Arthur in the sting was the man in the Hard Yakka work shirt at the service station, who also turned out to be a detective. Apparently he had drained petrol from her tank while she was at the reception to ensure she would stop at the servo.

Glancing at the familiar faces in a small interview room Sarah said, 'So this whole thing was a set up?'

Mike Arthur shook his head. 'No, not entirely. Senior Constable Morrison here really was getting married and she graciously agreed to let us work the investigation into her big day.'

Sarah shot Vanessa a look of pure venom. '*You* must have had an extreme makeover.'

'Yeah something like that,' Vanessa said. 'It's amazing what a nice suit and an hour with a hair and makeup artist can do. We didn't think you'd be too keen to have someone as working class as a police officer as a client.'

'You got that right,' Sarah agreed. 'And I'm guessing the car wasn't yours either?'

'Harold Tynes from European Luxury Cars was happy to assist us in our investigation,' Vanessa replied. 'Especially considering his daughter was your first victim.'

'And that dump really was your family home?'

Vanessa smiled coldly at Sarah before answering. 'Unlike you Ms Harris, I take great pride in my family and the way I was raised. Don't think I didn't notice the way you turned your nose up at the house. Oh yes, we've traced your background, and we know you were a scholarship student and those rich girls at Northill Grammar made your life hell. But that doesn't give you the right to steal.'

Sarah had honestly never considered what she did to be stealing. Rich people would not miss a pair of cufflinks here, a diamond necklace there, stray cash and the odd digital camera. Or so she'd thought. People were always so distracted on their daughter's wedding day that the photographer had access to anywhere in the house and Sarah was always amazed at just what was left lying around.

Detective Arthur spoke again. 'We've traced your little spree back four years and we've been close to catching you a couple of times, but getting your prints at the Morrison house and the footage from the hidden camera in the shed finally nailed you.'

'I'm surprised the fifty dollar notes weren't marked,' Sarah muttered.

'Well, they were actually,' Detective Arthur admitted. 'But you left such a convincing trail of evidence we didn't really need them after all.'

'I hope you've got a secondary career to fall back on,' Vanessa said.

'Huh?'

'Oh come on Ms Harris, don't play dumb. As talented as you are, I'm afraid you're finished in the photography business.'

In the end Sarah escaped a jail term, but was ordered to complete five hundred hours of community service and to make financial restitution to those she had stolen from. It was unfortunate that her case got so much publicity, because it ensured that, as Vanessa had so kindly pointed out, she was finished as a photographer.

Despite all she had been through over the months that had passed since her arrest, Sarah was grateful that the police investigation had not uncovered her other little side venture. Although she had been ordered to return all negatives and digital photograph DVDs to the brides she had stolen from, they hadn't said anything about the backup copies she kept in a self-storage shed.

As she packaged up another set of wedding photos she had sold at black market rates to a bridal magazine in the ever expanding Chinese market, Sarah couldn't help but smile.

• • • • •

Edith's eyes were wide when Grace finished reading.

'Sarah was a piece of work, wasn't she?' Grace began. 'She was so focused on outward appearances.'

Edith gave a slow nod.

'Yeah, she definitely was, but in a weird way I kind of understood her.'

Edith's expression changed enough for Grace to know she was asking her to elaborate. She had never realised before just how much you could communicate non-verbally.

'I'm not saying I agreed with what she did, I just meant when Vanessa made that comment about her being a scholarship girl I could sort of see how she ended up like that.'

Edith glanced at Grace curiously, studying her face intently. Grace could feel the flush spreading over her face and neck and travelling down her arms. She shook her head. 'Forget it,' she mumbled, 'I don't know what I'm saying.'

That intense look again and a tiny shake of Edith's head. Despite her discomfort Grace felt it would be rude not to keep talking and took a second to gather her thoughts.

'Well a scholarship sounds like a great thing. I mean it gives a person an opportunity to do something that would otherwise be beyond their grasp. But sometimes … well, sometimes other people don't like it.'

Edith was still looking at her.

'It shouldn't matter but in some places it does,' Grace said. 'Or so I've heard,' she added quietly.

Edith nodded again and gave an expression that Grace couldn't quite decipher. Not wanting to take the topic any further, Grace changed tack. 'I think it's time to move on to theme and setting,' she murmured, picking up the book again and avoiding Edith's gaze as she did so.

Grace heard it as soon as she entered the hallway from Edith's room. It was faint but unmistakable – piano music. She hadn't noticed a piano either time she'd come in but clearly there was one somewhere on the premises. It got louder as she sped towards the exit, desperate to leave before the beauty of the melody found a chink in her armour and enticed her to stop and absorb the music.

Although Grace did her best not to listen, her brain betrayed her, feeding her signals about what she was hearing. The pianist was clearly an amateur, missing the b flat on the base chords and was too heavy on the pedal, but for the purpose of entertaining elderly folk in a nursing home it was good music. The piano was one of those compact upright ones and it badly needed a tune, but Grace guessed it probably wasn't high on the priority list when so many other things needed to be done on a day-to-day basis.

Grace hadn't realised she was standing still until the maintenance man appeared in front of her, lugging a huge floor polishing machine. 'Sorry,' he said as he leant over and plugged it in, 'this will block out the music. You can go down to the rec room and listen if you like.'

'It's all right,' Grace assured him, 'I really have to go.' Not caring how strange she looked, she ran down the hallway and out the nearest door.

* * * * *

Leaving her home and all that was familiar to her had been a wrench but Grace had embraced the opportunity to attend her final year of high school at the exclusive Strauss Musical Academy. Being there as a result of the generosity of others she was ever mindful that she needed to be the best she could possibly be to pay them back for their belief in her.

As nervous as she was, Grace was determined to make the most of every advantage the exclusive musical academy offered. Coming in so late in her schooling she knew it would be difficult to fit in and had even decided she could make it through the year without friends if the other kids didn't accept a small town country girl crashing their scene.

In reality it had turned out much better than expected. Grace made friends easily and didn't feel like an outsider for long. Having a car, and such a nice new one at that, gave her status. And by wearing the same uniform as everybody else, nobody had to know that she could not afford the designer labels the other girls wore off campus.

She had feared resentment going straight in as the lead pianist but soon realised that her talent as a pianist was why she had been accepted into the academy in the first place. The previous girl had withdrawn unexpectedly and they needed somebody of the same calibre – or even better if what her tutor told her was true – to fill her shoes and maintain the integrity of their orchestra.

Best of all though Grace just loved being around people who loved music as much as she did.

Grace loathed being late. She hated the idea of people waiting expectantly and disappointing them by not showing up at an agreed time. So even though her lack of punctuality on her third visit was caused by road works on the access road and was not actually her fault she still felt guilty as she rushed through the complex. Hoping Edith wouldn't be upset she hurried through the east wing and skidded to a halt outside Room 46.

After opening the door and bustling inside in a way that was very out of character for her, Grace stopped short at what greeted her. Shocked she shook her head to clear her vision to determine if the scene before her was real or imagined.

Edith's hair (or was it a wig? Grace still wasn't sure) was piled on top of her head and pinned in an elaborate arrangement, with soft curls unravelling down over her shoulders. Her makeup was bold today, darker than she normally wore it and her nails were blood red. Rather than her bed jacket, she was dressed in a delicate coral negligee. Grace stifled a gasp at the stark reality of Edith's frailty, how thin her shoulders and arms were and how translucent and mottled her skin.

Trying hard not to stare Grace could tell that Edith was intrigued by her discomfiture. Yet again, she was unsure how to react. She felt desperately sorry for Edith, living the life she did, but that was normal wasn't it? Was this some kind of test to determine if she was a tolerant person?

'Hello,' Grace finally said.

'Like the getup?'

Grace almost jumped out of her skin, but soon realised the voice was coming from the bathroom and not from

Edith. Peering around the door she found a cleaner inside. 'You scared me,' she accused, too wound up with the events of the morning to be polite.

The cleaner chuckled heartily. 'Sorry,' she said as she came back into the room. 'But you should see the look on your face.'

The flush that enveloped Grace was a mixture of annoyance and embarrassment. 'Well it was a bit of a shock,' she said. 'I mean it's different to what Edith normally wears.'

'There's no rule saying you have to wear the same thing day in, day out.'

Grace flushed deeper. 'Yes I realise that. I'm not saying she can't wear it, I'm just a bit confused…'

'Yes I know love, it's not the norm. I'm Marion,' she said, holding out her hand. Tall and slightly plump she had a kind, motherly face.

'Grace,' Grace responded. 'Is there a special occasion or something?'

'Kind of. Edith has always wanted one of those glamour photography shots, so Sylvia arranged it for her.'

'Wow. I didn't know you could do that here.'

'What, you don't think someone in a nursing home can doll themselves up for some flash pictures? Trust me Grace, they don't care where you come from or how you look, they only care if your money is good.'

Grace shook her head. 'No, no I wasn't saying that, I just thought you had to go to a studio or something.'

'No they've got portable equipment and will go all over the place. The photographer had never been to a nursing home before but was very accommodating.'

'Oh, okay. Wow.'

Marion shook her head. 'I know what you're thinking – why bother? What's the point?'

'No, no I wasn't,' Grace protested, mortified that Edith might be offended by that statement, which she was ashamed to admit had crossed her mind.

Marion busied herself dusting the wheelchair and moving it back into place. 'The photographer used a green screen to hide all the background stuff and they'll do their magic with Photoshop. Edith is going to use it on her Christmas card.'

'Wow, that will be nice,' Grace said, knowing how condescending she must sound.

'Yes it will,' agreed Marion, winking at Edith. 'And she can tick it off her bucket list too.'

Grace didn't know where to look. Talking about bucket lists in a nursing home seemed to be in very poor taste. Catching a glimpse of her face, Marion winked at Edith again and burst into laughter. Edith gave one of her lopsided grins.

Ready to spontaneously combust with embarrassment, Grace could only smile insincerely in return and busy herself looking for the book.

Margaret woke long before her alarm. She'd set it for 6.15 am to give herself plenty of time to get organised and run through everything in her head one more time. Seeing it was only 5.45 Margaret stretched contentedly, savouring the cosy feeling between sleep and wakefulness for a moment, before a feeling of dread enveloped her.

The day had finally come.

Trying to ignore the churning in her stomach, Margaret rolled over and flicked on the bedside radio. Unfortunately, the chirpy banter of the breakfast show hosts did little to distract her. In desperation she took some deep, cleansing breaths the way she had learned at her yoga class. It helped a little. But as Margaret listened to the news and weather, it seemed unfair that the world was going on in its usual way while she was so stressed out.

As Margaret stood under the shower she wondered again why she was putting herself through this ordeal. Her old life had been safe and far less demanding and for a moment she wished she was back there. Her husband Mick was away on a work conference and it would be easy enough to go back to bed and watch the *Today* show like she used to each morning.

Nobody will think any the less of me if I don't keep at it, she reassured herself as she rinsed the conditioner out of her hair. It was probably just a crazy mid-life crisis idea I should never have acted on.

Stepping out of the shower she eyed herself sternly in the mirror over the sink, remembering how long it had taken her to step out of her comfort zone.

'You're going Margaret and that's that!' she said firmly and set about getting ready.

The silence in the kitchen was suffocating. Although Mick always left for work early, her daughter Karen usually ate breakfast with her. But today *would* be the day she had a personal training session before work. This was one morning that Margaret could have used some of Karen's calm reassurance.

Glancing at the clock, Margaret nibbled a slice of vegemite toast and forced herself to drink her tea. It wouldn't do her any good to leave the house without something in her stomach. She remembered how Karen and her other daughter Lisa used to complain that they couldn't eat when they were nervous and she had told them it was all in their minds. Now she understood what they meant.

Margaret's hands were shaking as she packed her bag and she wavered once again. It's not natural to be so stressed she fretted. Maybe it's my instincts telling me I'm not cut out for all this. I'm still in the grace period, so there's no penalty if I pull out now. Turning towards the picture window she glanced out at the perfectly manicured garden and sighed wearily. As much as she loved her garden and didn't regret the time she had put into it, she had always known it was an avoidance tactic, an excuse not to act on what her heart was yearning to do.

Picking up her bag Margaret strode purposefully towards the front door and whatever fate may await her that day.

Doing her best to look calm and composed, Margaret walked down her street, head held high. Barbara on the corner gave her a wave and a smile. 'Gosh don't you look the part?' she called out cheerily. 'You're much braver than me Marg!'

Margaret smiled back but didn't stop to chat. She

supposed it *was* quite brave to enrol at university at the age of forty-six. Although it *had* taken years of deliberation before she even considered applying and she had dithered for days before accepting her place when it was offered.

After a bit of a shaky start Margaret felt she was finally starting to find her feet. She knew her way around the campus and how to use the library. And there were many other mature age students at the University of Queensland, so she didn't stand out like she had feared she would. Most of the younger students were friendly and respectful and Margaret had struck up a few friendships already.

Yes, uni in general was going just fine. It was only Introductory Poetry that had her tied up in knots, all thanks to Professor Bernstein. His reputation as a tyrant who struck fear into the hearts of meek first year students had unfortunately proven to be correct. Upon hearing Margaret had struck him Karen couldn't contain her sympathy. 'Oh Mum, you poor thing,' she'd wailed. 'Remember my friend Jasmine?'

'The thin redheaded girl?'

'Uh, huh.'

'I remember she used to cry a lot when you were in first year.'

'Yeah, well that was all because of Berno. She blitzed English at school, but he terrified her. He failed two thirds of her class on one assignment and he *never* gave anyone higher than a credit.'

'Right,' Margaret murmured, feeling a little faint. Maybe she could just drop poetry. But that would be silly.

The whole reason she was going to uni was to learn about poetry.

Despite her best attempts to keep an open mind about Professor Bernstein, Margaret soon realised his reputation preceded him for a reason. A tall, stooped man with thick curly grey hair, his imposing presence filled every corner of the huge lecture hall. Strictly old school, he refused to wear a microphone, relying instead on his booming voice to put his point across.

Margaret didn't doubt the professor was a poetic genius, but it was hard to appreciate his brilliance when she was so scared of him. It wasn't so bad in the lecture, because there were a hundred other students there and you could hide up the back away from his steely gaze. It was the tutorials that terrified Margaret most. There were only fourteen students and Professor Bernstein, in a tiny room with nowhere to hide. She had bluffed her way through the first two tutes, but this week was different. Her class had handed in an introductory assignment to allow Professor Bernstein to judge their ability level and he was going to speak to each of them individually to discuss their results.

As an M surname Margaret was right in the middle of the class list and today was Wednesday.

D Day.

Compulsively early for everything, Margaret did her best to dawdle but still made it to the bus stop in plenty of time. And yes, today would be the day the bus arrived right on cue. Taking a seat, Margaret couldn't help feeling like she should be doing something else to prepare herself for the day ahead.

Opening her bag she pulled out a dog-eared copy of her assignment and read through it again, making sure she knew exactly what she had written, should the professor decide to grill her.

Have I even answered the question? Turning the pages over, she read it again. *Why has poetry continued to survive as a valid form of prose in a technological world?*

Margaret knew there was no such thing as a "right" answer; that the strength of an assignment was in the argument you presented. Despite spending three solid days working on it she still didn't believe her answer would satisfy Professor Bernstein. Once the initial relief of handing her work in faded, Margaret now cringed every time she imagined him reading it.

The melodic tone of her mobile phone sounded and the screen display showed that it was Karen on the line.

'Hello,' Margaret answered softly, determined not to be one of those annoying passengers who conducted loud mobile phone conversations.

'Hi Mum, I just wanted to ring and see that you weren't still stressing about seeing old Berno today.'

'Well, uh, no, not really.'

'Chill Mum, he can't kill you,' Karen reassured her. 'I know I put the wind up you when I told you about Jasmine, but she was really a bit of a drama queen. You're just another student to him and a first year at that. He's not stressing about your meeting, so you shouldn't worry about it either.'

'Oh I wish I had your confidence,'

Sitting outside Professor Bernstein's office before her meeting, Margaret chatted nervously to a fellow student named Kirsty who was awaiting the same fate. Margaret wished she could be as calm and unruffled as this seventeen year old, who was chewing gum and filing her nails.

'Aren't you nervous?' Margaret asked, trying to quell the butterflies in her stomach.

'Nah, old Berno doesn't worry me,' Kirsty replied. 'This is only worth ten per cent, and besides you've got until week six to drop out or change subjects.'

Margaret smiled politely and gnawed at her thumbnail, which was now bitten down to the quick. It was a nervous habit from her childhood that the nuns at her school had never managed to curb.

Kirsty handed Margaret her emery board. 'Really, I think you're getting yourself too worked up about this.'

Margaret nodded her thanks and filed her ragged nail. Maybe she *was* over-reacting. But what if Professor Bernstein told her she was no good at writing? How would she face him at the tutorial each week? Oh why did I ever think this was a good idea?

The low murmur of conversation inside the office was punctuated by an angry raised voice. Although they couldn't hear what was being said, Margaret and Kirsty exchanged a nervous glance. Now Margaret could detect fear on the teenager's face.

'Really, his bark is worse than his bite,' Kirsty insisted

as she fiddled with the end of her plait.

The door to Professor Bernstein's office opened suddenly. Margaret looked up with a start as a short wiry boy walked out clutching an assignment covered in red ink. The terrified look on his face said it all. Kirsty gulped audibly and Margaret wondered if she had time to dash to the toilet again.

'Next,' barked the voice from inside the office.

Margaret scuttled in with her head down and perched on the edge of the visitor's chair. About sixty years old, Professor Bernstein was wearing brown trousers that looked to be at least a decade past their prime, a white shirt that had gone grey in the wash and an ugly paisley tie. Reading glasses were perched on the end of his nose and the legendary beady eyes that had scared so many students over the years didn't even look up from the pile of assignments in front of him.

'Margaret McCormick?' he snapped gruffly.

Margaret bit her lip. 'Yes that's right,' she squeaked.

Professor Bernstein picked up her assignment and made a great show of leafing through it, saying 'mmm' several times and pausing dramatically each time he turned the page.

'Well, Margaret clearly it has been some time since you were at school.'

Margaret's stomach clenched. This was going to be worse than she had imagined. Her lack of knowledge about poetry must have been *very* obvious in her writing.

'Yes it's been a few years,' she replied, her voice still

squeaky.

'I know people think I'm an old fool but I can always pick a more mature student's work as opposed to those young louts who breeze through the doors these days barely able to spell their own names.'

'Oh, right,' said Margaret, very unsure where this was leading.

'You see Margaret, you are one of the few students in this class who appears to have any kind of grip on the English language. Your argument is too hesitant and you could have explored some of the concepts raised to a higher level, but on the whole this was a passable effort.'

The sense of relief that flowed through Margaret was like the rush of adrenaline that accompanies a near miss with another car on the highway.

'That's good to hear,' she answered, her voice almost back to its normal pitch.

'So where *did* you go to school?'

'St Anthony's.'

Professor Bernstein raised his bushy eyebrows and eyed Margaret closely. 'Really? Here in Brisbane?'

Margaret nodded, noting the immediate softening of the professor's expression. He looked almost friendly!

'My mother was the Senior English Mistress there for twenty-five years!' Professor Bernstein exclaimed. 'You know, I can always spot somebody who was taught to her exacting standards.'

'Yes, of course, Mrs Bernstein. Well what a small world it is!'

'Indeed, indeed. My dear mother – may she rest in

peace – was the one who inspired me to go on and study English. She was such a gentle woman and so caring of her students. Firm but kind and she always got results. Just look at you, out of school for many years and still served well by Mum's wonderful teaching. It was far superior to the young teachers of today, who in my humble opinion, are much too liberal.'

Professor Bernstein handed Margaret back her essay with a warm smile that softened his stern face. Margaret could only sit and grin in relief as her heart slowed to its normal speed.

'Like I said Margaret, you need to be a bit more assertive in your writing but that will come with experience. I don't expect you to have any problems in my course.'

Margaret just smiled again, thanked the professor and left his office before he changed his mind.

Karen laughed as Margaret relayed the story back to her that afternoon over a cup of tea. 'Fancy you being taught by old Berno's mother and him being able to pick up on it like that. He's obviously not as out of touch as he appears to be.'

Margaret smiled. 'Ah but I wasn't taught by her. Remember I left school when I was fifteen so I didn't do senior English at St Anthony's.'

'Oh, so you lied to get into Berno's good books,' Karen replied with a mock stern look.

Margaret shook her head and took another sip of tea. 'No I didn't lie. I just let Professor Bernstein draw his own conclusions, inaccurate as they may be.'

Karen chuckled again. 'Fair enough. So what was she like?'

'Does the fact that her nickname was Battleaxe Bernstein answer your question?'

'I take it you didn't tell her adoring son that?'

'No definitely not,' Margaret chuckled. 'I may be new at this whole uni thing, but I do know to quit while I'm ahead.'

Karen broke a Scotch finger biscuit in half and dunked one piece in her tea. 'So, who should really get the credit for your superior English skills?'

'Well here's a laugh for you. I went back and did most of my senior subjects at night when you girls were little. All except English. I only did that two years ago to qualify for uni and my teacher was a twenty-two-year-old new graduate.'

'No!' Karen exclaimed. 'Seriously?'

'Uh huh. So much for the liberal young teachers of today, hey?'

Margaret and Karen looked at each other again and burst into laughter.

• • • • •

Initially, Grace felt self-conscious reading the story with Marion in the room. She had dawdled for a while, flicking through the pages slowly to get to the right place and wriggled in the lumpy chair to get as comfortable as possible, but had eventually realised the other woman had no intention of leaving. Deciding to just get on with it, she soon lost herself in the reading of the story, so much so that she was startled when Marion chuckled heartily at the conclusion.

'I enjoyed that,' she said as she dusted the pictures on the wall. 'You've got a real knack for reading aloud.'

'Thanks,' Grace said.

'I was out at UQ for many years myself.'

Grace couldn't hide her surprise. 'Oh, really? What did you study?'

'Not a thing!' Marion laughed. 'I used to clean there.'

'Oh right. Did you ever wish you were a student?'

Marion looked up from where she was cleaning Edith's dressing table. 'Maybe once or twice, but believe it or not I'm very happy with my career.'

'Oh.'

Marion arched an eyebrow. 'Did *you* go to uni? Or do you still go? You're about the right age.'

Grace hesitate a second and then shook her head. 'No, no I haven't ever been to uni.'

'What about TAFE or another training college?'

'No.'

The silence hung between them a moment and Grace could see that Edith was following the conversation with interest. 'I don't really work at the moment,' she said eventually. 'I'm just sorting some stuff out, you know.'

'Looking for your true vocation, huh?'

'Uh, yeah,' Grace replied, while desperately searching for a conversation topic away from her vocation or gross lack thereof. Looking back at Edith she smiled a little forcefully and picked up the book again. 'Sorry, we're getting off topic here. Uh, I really liked the way Margaret was thinking on her feet,' she finally blurted. 'I mean she was really scared and everything but she really picked up on the way the Professor got all wistful when he spoke about his mother and she said something that scored her some brownie points.'

'Yeah, she did and then of course we realise she was fudging it a bit – although as she said herself she didn't lie, she just let the professor draw his own conclusion.' Marion seemed determined to continue involving herself in the conversation.

'Lying by omission,' Grace said.

'Mmmm, kind of,' Marion agreed. 'I don't know that that is always a bad thing. Take Margaret for example, nobody was hurt and there was little likelihood of being found out given that Mrs Bernstein is dead. So all she did was use a lever to put herself in the best place to succeed with her study.'

'That's true.'

'And, besides the Professor had already told her she had a good writing style before she told him where she went to school, so it's not like he totally changed his opinion of her.'

'Yeah.'

Marion was rearranging Edith's drawers now. Grace suspected it was a delaying tactic but knew she couldn't very well ask her to leave. Besides, maybe it was interesting for Edith to have another opinion in the mix.

'Let's face it we're all guilty of lying by omission sometimes,' Marion said.

Grace froze for a moment, then forced herself to nod her head. 'Yes,' she replied softly, willing the fleeting image to only skim the rim of her conscious mind and not settle there.

Detecting the change in Grace, Marion steered the conversation back to safer waters. 'So what do you think the moral of the story was?'

Grace was determined to be positive. 'It's never too late to try something new.'

'Good advice that.'

The road works were still in progress as Grace made her way home; in fact the workers had expanded what they were doing. Huge chunks of bitumen had been ripped up and they appeared to be replacing a water main. Noticing the detour signs Grace realised she was going to have to take an alternative route. Damn she thought, what was the point of having a safeguarding system when it could be upset so easily?

As she drove the long way home Grace kept her eyes straight ahead. But it was no use. Even if she didn't physically look over at the Conservatorium she knew it was there, doing what it had always done. Grace sighed sadly wondering if she would ever be able to look at it without feeling such an aching loss.

It was hard to fathom that she should be graduating this year. Grace scrupulously avoided the musical circles she used to move in, having no wish to hear about the successes of her former classmates as they made their way into the performing world. It was just too painful to contemplate what might have been … what *should* have been if her life hadn't derailed along the way.

* * * * *

Unlike almost most other high school seniors, the pupils at Strauss did not have to stress about their immediate future. Part of its exclusivity was the pathway program it provided – guaranteeing every graduating student a place at either the Conservatorium of Music or a degree in music at any university of their choice. Naturally they did have to fulfil their other academic requirements as well, but they were so well monitored and supported with their studies it was almost impossible to fail.

Grace had kept her options open, applying to uni as well as contemplating the Con. She had always liked the idea of teaching music as well as performing and knew it was easy enough to complete her Bachelor of Education as a combined degree. While it would be amazing to be surrounded by other musicians as passionate as her at the conservatorium, no doubt there would be a lot of pressure as well, not to mention fairly serious competitiveness. The less structured environment at uni that wasn't exclusively about music did hold a certain amount of appeal.

She had to admit that she had felt a little smug compared to her friends from home who were still dithering about whether or not to continue studying and if so what course to take. It was a relief to have all that sorted out and just focus on the endless opportunities Strauss provided.

If anybody had asked, Grace would never have said it was *easy* for her to get in her car and travel to Rosehill Gardens each week. But she had to admit it was becoming less difficult. The drive there was no longer such a tense experience, and rather than clenching the steering wheel struggling for control and psyching herself up for what was to come, Grace found herself looking forward to seeing Edith and interested in the story they might read that day.

I almost feel normal, Grace realised as she exited onto the access road. I'm going somewhere and I've got something to do. It wasn't like having a proper job – Grace had accepted that was not to be her path in life – but it felt good. She was doing something with her time that actually meant something both to her and another person. Although still of the opinion the Rejoin program was ultimately not going to be of benefit to her, she conceded that it did have some merit.

Edith was dozing when Grace arrived, so she closed the door quietly and sat down. Making herself as comfortable as she could in the lumpy chair Grace studied the room. As much as Edith had personalised it, like no other room at Rosehill, it was still a small space that spoke little of the sum of Edith's life experiences. The photographs on the wall showed a younger, mobile Edith who was clearly an adventurous soul. A multi-shot frame displayed action shots of that other woman horse riding, sky diving and aboard a yacht holding a glass of champagne. How does all that energy and purpose fizzle to nothing? How does a healthy, even curvaceous body shrivel to skin and bone?

Caught up in her wondering, Grace was startled when she glanced up and found Edith watching her intently.

'Sorry,' she murmured, 'I wasn't being a stalker or anything.'

Edith's expression was mild. She raised her eyebrows as if to say 'no problem'.

'You look like you had a lot of fun back when you could … uh before...'

A blink and a smile.

'I think I've forgotten how to have fun,' Grace admitted. 'It's kind of strange, you don't think about it when you're a kid, you just do stuff you like and play and it all seems like fun. But then you grow up and you realise the world isn't always a nice place and you kind of forget about having fun.'

Edith eyed her intently, so much so that Grace felt she should explain herself further. 'But it's different when you're a grown up isn't it? I mean if you like daring kind of things like the pictures here, I guess that's fun. But I'm not daring, so my options are a bit limited.'

Edith just kept looking at her and this time her eyes were definitely sad.

Rosie, Bev, Ross and Scott greeted each other with little enthusiasm outside SmallWorld IT Solutions at 8.30 am on December thirty-first. All the other business car parks remained empty; and the street that was usually bustling with traffic was deserted. It appeared that they were the only people who had to work on New Year's Eve.

'Would you look at the colour of that sky,' said Rosie wistfully, her mind still back at the beach house where she had spent the last week. The other three peered upwards into the cerulean depths and agreed that it was a crime to waste a summer sky like that by being indoors.

None of them had worked on December thirty-first at SmallWorld before. Like the other businesses in the industrial estate it used to remain closed between Christmas and New Year. Yes, they had all heard the stories from Mr Small each year about how his holiday had been interrupted because he was always gracious enough to be on call, but they never imagined that he would pass on the responsibility to somebody else this year.

They had all protested when Mr Small had announced the crew rostered to work New Year's Eve. Each of them told him how inconvenient it was to come in for one day and that they had other plans. But Mr Small was unmoved. Unless there was a valid excuse that could be verified, they were rostered on to work. He reminded the quartet that they were being paid double time and would enjoy a pub lunch at company expense. None of them felt this was worthy compensation for having to be in the office on a day when the rest of the country (and more specifically the rest of their workmates) were out having fun.

For security reasons a minimum of four staff had to be present and Mr Small had chosen each of them for a specific reason. Rosie had the keys and alarm codes, Ross was the most experienced senior technician, Scott was the resident virus removal expert and for Bev it was an opportunity to run the end of year invoices without the hassle of having to backdate them.

Rosie extracted a bulky key ring from her bulging, oversized handbag. As the office manager she sometimes felt that she had all the responsibilities of being the boss without any of the privileges or financial reward. She worked her way through the series of locks and disarmed the alarm, then held the door open for her workmates to enter.

The first through the door was Bev who sighed in disapproval as she turned on the lights and surveyed the state of the office. Empty beer bottles littered a few of the desktops and chip packets lay on the floor along with a pile of crushed Styrofoam cups. Dirty dishes were haphazardly stacked in the small kitchen sink and a noticeable stench emanated from the overflowing rubbish bin. Giving a 'tsk' of annoyance, Bev headed for her locker to stow her bag. Although her official role was accounts clerk, Bev considered herself to also be the unofficial maid, as nobody else seemed to be capable of even basic cleaning tasks.

Ross headed straight for his desk. He had been one of the last to leave the Christmas Eve drinks and had vague, unsettling memories of taking photos of various staff members that seemed like a lot of fun at the time, but might well be considered inappropriate in the cold light of day when dead sober. As one of the system administrators at least he had the ability to get them off his hard drive and off the office network in case they had found their way on to it.

Scott went into the storeroom and wheeled out the portable TV into the communal workspace area. Plugging it in, he began fiddling with the rabbit's ears antenna and eventually tuned into Channel 9. As long as they were stuck here for the day, they should at least be able to see what was happening at the Gabba. If he were at home he wouldn't have missed a minute of the cricket on TV or better still could have joined his mates at the Gabba to soak up the atmosphere of the match, along with a few beers.

Eyeing her cluttered workspace, Rosie sighed wearily. It was always so easy to waltz out of the office on Christmas Eve full of cheer and unconcerned about what you were leaving behind. Facing the mess on your first day back was another thing altogether.

Eventually she decided to address the staff. 'Okay guys, I know none of us want to be here, but we are so let's try and have a productive day. I'm not saying we have to work at full capacity but we'll need something to show for being here for eight hours.'

First Rosie gave Bev a hand restoring the kitchen to order as Scott collected the empty beer bottles from the main work area. As much as Mr Small seemed to think they would be swamped with calls from people whose hard drives had crashed or who had opened a suspicious email and come under a viral attack, the phone hadn't rung yet so she had plenty of time to get her own work done later.

'I suppose you've got big plans for tonight,' said Bev as she handed Rosie a plate to dry.

Listening to the details of Rosie's action packed weekends was a Monday lunch tradition for most of the staff at SmallWorld. They all agreed it must be hard for her to fit work in around her social life. Bev knew that Rosie would surely be out until the sun rose on THE party night of the year.

'Oh yeah,' Rosie agreed. 'Too many invites and not enough time! I'll narrow it down by this afternoon. Southbank is always fun … or Surfers or Mooloolaba even. I don't suppose I'll have time to get on a flight to Sydney,' she added. 'The fireworks there are always amazing.'

Shaking her head at the very idea of flying to another city on the spur of the moment, Bev said, 'I envy you young single women of today. You've got the freedom to go out and do what you like without the stigma of spinsterhood that my generation was saddled with.'

'Yeah I guess we do,' Rosie said with a smile as she attempted to stack the plates back into the crowded cupboard above the sink. 'How about you?' Rosie asked. 'Do you and Ed host a big neighbourhood bash or anything?'

Bev couldn't help but chuckle as she scrubbed the coffee stains out of a white mug. 'No, no nothing like that. We've always taken New Year's Eve quietly, instead of getting caught up in those big crowds. We'll be in bed by ten as usual and get up early to see the sun rise tomorrow.'

'Each to their own,' Rosie said, hanging up her tea towel to dry and looking around the clean kitchen. 'There, that wasn't so bad after all. It's always easier to do the dishes when you've got company.'

'Thanks Rosie, you're absolutely right,' Bev said as she let the water out of the sink and wiped down the bench. 'I can concentrate on those invoices now that I've got this all sorted out.'

Ross was the only one hard at work. Unfortunately, the

work he was doing was putting out fires – yes, fires that he had started. He decided that next time he intended to drink at an office function he would remove the power cable from his computer before the party started and lock it in the office safe. Ross couldn't believe he had managed to wreak so much havoc with the internal office email when he was so drunk. How had he even remembered his passwords let alone the complex steps required to create a file share?

While his workmates were distracted by other chores, Ross cleared the offending photos off the network and set about deleting the emails he had forwarded to all staff. This could only be done if the emails were unopened, so he had to work quickly. Preoccupied with the task at hand he jumped in fright when Scott appeared at his desk.

'Geez mate, you scared the living daylights out of me. You shouldn't sneak up on people like that.'

'I wasn't sneaking; I called out to you twice. What's got you so busy over here anyway?'

Ross managed to minimise the screen he was working on before it was in Scott's line of vision. 'A rogue email slipped through the firewall, I'm just deleting it,' he replied casually, hoping to stall Scott before he had a chance to check his inbox. 'What's news anyway? Any nasty Christmas viruses we should know about?'

Scott sat on a nearby desk. 'No not really. The drunken Santa attachment was the worst of them and that was contained pretty well before Christmas Eve. I've only had one call. The guy said he was desperate until I told him the callout fee, then he said he could wait until Monday and bring it in here.'

'People have got other things on their minds today; they're gearing up for a big night,' Ross said as he surreptitiously binned the last of the offending emails.

Scott scrunched a piece of paper into a ball then tossed and caught it. Well known around the office as a cricket fanatic he was always throwing, bowling or batting something. 'So,' he said casually, 'what are you up to tonight? Footloose and fancy free, you must have big plans?'

'Oh you know me Scott, lead me somewhere where there's plenty of alcohol and I'll be happy as Larry. Goodness knows where I'll wake up tomorrow morning, or who with.'

Feeling a great sense of relief now that all the photos were deleted, Ross leaned back in his chair and put his feet up on the desk. 'What about you? That lovely young wife of yours taking you out on the town?'

Scott continued to throw and catch the paper ball. 'No, it'll be a quiet one for me. Lara is working a night shift, so I'm staying home in solidarity. It's no fun to party hard without her there anyway.'

Ross's eyebrows shot up. 'You really mean that? You'd rather stay home alone than have a big night without your wife?'

'Absolutely.'

'Wow, you young blokes have got it all worked out. I bet that line of thinking earns you lots of brownie points.'

'Oh yes, it has its compensations all right,' Scott agreed.

The morning ambled on slowly, punctuated by an occasional phone call, including from a few staff members who wanted to gloat.

'Actually we're having a great day here,' Rosie said to her workmate Siobhan. 'We're sitting around watching the cricket and getting paid for it.'

'Yeah right,' Siobhan laughed. 'You couldn't have paid me enough to come into work today. I'm halfway through a bottle of wine, lying in a hammock – no amount of money can make up for that.'

'That may well be true, but today will pay off half my credit card bill,' Rosie countered.

'I'm not even thinking about that yet,' Siobhan said. 'I'll let you get back to the *cricket*,' she added. 'What's the score by the way?'

'Not sure, there's an ad break on,' Rosie said briskly before hanging up. She knew she shouldn't let Siobhan needle her and she should consider it a compliment that Mr Small trusted her enough to run the show in his absence, but she would trade it all in a second to be back at the beach.

That wasn't going to happen though and Rosie finally got stuck into her work. Within the hour she had her desk tidied, filing done and her emails up to date. Checking around the office the other staff were apparently just as productive. Bev had the end of month invoices run and ready for mailing. Ross was talking someone through using a system restore point over the phone and Scott was undertaking simple virus removal jobs on machines that had been left in the workshop, all the while keeping one eye on the cricket.

Just before twelve they headed to the nearby pub for lunch. Rosie diverted the office phone to her mobile, but didn't expect too many calls. They each ordered a drink from the bar and then selected a table in the corner, away from the noise of the pool tables and poker machines.

'Getting started on your New Year festivities early?' the young waitress asked cheerily, as she handed out the menus and pointed out the specials board. 'Isn't it great to work days so we can all go out and party the night away?'

They all nodded eagerly.

Picking up her menu, Rosie grinned wickedly. 'Order whatever you like guys. Smally can afford it.'

Bev walked over to the counter to study the specials board. Looking around the crowded pub and feeling the festive atmosphere she sighed deeply. As she had told Rosie, she and Ed never made a fuss about New Year's Eve but the truth was she would *love* to sample it, just once. Marrying in her early twenties and having her family young meant that at the age of fifty-one she now had all the time in the world for a social life but no real opportunity. She loved Ed, she really did, he was a kind, considerate, hardworking man. He just liked a quiet life and believed that a night out at the RSL once a week was more than enough socialising.

Bev didn't want to go out and get drunk or join the teeming crowds at Southbank, but it would be nice to be out somewhere, just doing something to mark the occasion. Deciding on the mixed grill – same as she always had – Bev went back to the table ready to continue her façade of a quiet New Year's Eve by choice.

Ross sipped his light beer and resisted the temptation to order a double scotch. He didn't think Rosie would make that much of a fuss if he did, but given that he did have plans to get spectacularly drunk that night, he knew he should pace himself.

He had given Scott the impression that he was going out somewhere to write himself off, but in reality he had no plans to leave his house. It would be too pathetic. New Year's Eve had been his wedding anniversary for fifteen years and he and his wife had always hosted a big party. Recently separated, he had hoped that his children might at least want to spend some time with him, but their mother had taken them to Noosa instead. 'It will be a chance for them to create some new, *positive* memories,' she had informed him nastily the previous week.

Okay, he could admit that the last few NYE bashes had seen him get a little out of control. But between his brother Rick and his neighbour Eddie, he had to keep up. It wasn't like he *deliberately* dropped the horrifically expensive, special order white chocolate mud cake face down onto the concrete last year. And, yes, in hindsight, throwing a chunk of the cake into the crowd and yelling 'food fight!' was not his best idea ever. Then again it wasn't as if they could eat it. As for throwing his wife's boss into the pool, well, of course he wouldn't have done that if he had known she couldn't swim.

Ross put down his beer and turned his attention to the

menu. Given that he had skipped breakfast and would not be eating that night he chose the seafood basket, which was huge. At least he would have some nutrition for the day.

When the waitress came back over to take their orders she looked closely at Scott. 'Aren't you Lara's boyfriend?' she asked.

'Husband actually,' Scott replied proudly. 'You're Nicky right?'

'Yes that's me. Lara and I were at school together, but I didn't know she got married. Wow, that must be nice, you've got a built in social life when you're a couple, none of the angst of the single life.'

'Too true,' Scott replied cheerily, hoping he sounded believable.

As a young newlywed he had taken it for granted that *the* social night of the year would be sorted this year. He had smugly believed that he and Lara could go on a romantic getaway somewhere and enjoy whatever NYE festivities were on offer there. Unfortunately, that plan had died when Lara's roster came out. His plan B to catch up with his single friends had also been shot down.

Of course he had told Ross he was staying home in solidarity, but it wasn't a question of solidarity, more of survival. Lara had bluntly spelled out the consequences if he went out drinking and having fun while she 'slaved away in a grotty hospital Emergency Department filled with idiots who couldn't hold their booze.' He had learned very early in his marriage that it was not acceptable for him to enjoy himself while his wife did shift work.

Keen to take the spotlight off himself and his social life, he asked Nicky if he could have wedges with his steak sandwich instead of chips.

'I'll see what I can do,' she said.

After Nicky left, the four workmates looked at each other a little shyly. It was a bit weird but outside the confines of the office they weren't sure what to say to each other. There had been other office lunches of course and parties, but never just the four of them together in a social setting.

Rosie broke the ice. 'So Scott, is it true that you gave up your dreams of playing cricket for Australia to come and work at SmallWorld?'

Scott laughed. 'Oh yeah, it was the hardest choice of my life. I mean a six figure salary and lots of first class travel around the world is all well and good, but it's not a long term career like the IT business.'

The other three laughed and looked at their workmate with interest. Scott was always so quiet and unassuming, they had never realised he had a sense of humour.

As lunch wore on and the workmates became more relaxed, confidences began to be exchanged.

'At my interview I told Mr Small I was very experienced with Rapid Pay which was a little bit of an exaggeration,' Rosie confessed. 'Then the next week he puts me in charge of setting it up for the company!'

'What did you do?' Bev asked. 'I remember you had it up and running in no time.'

'I sub-contracted it out to another firm,' she said with a grin. 'It cost me my first two months' salary, but Mr Small never realised. Given that nobody else knew anything about it, I could just faff around and act like I knew what I was doing. And I managed to offload that job over to you quick smart Bev.'

'Yes you did,' said Bev with a knowing smile.

'Well played Rosie.' Ross smiled and held his beer aloft.

Rosie clinked her glass against Ross' before looking around the table. 'All right guys come on, I've owned up to something now you have to as well.'

Scott spoke up first. 'Remember the Dracula virus that ran rampant about two years ago? Well I was the one who let it through. One of my idiot friends forwarded it and I unthinkingly opened it. Luckily it never got traced back to me.'

Ross stared at him in shock. 'Man I worked overtime for two weeks to fix that sucker! You're lucky it scrambled everything so badly it covered your tracks. Smally would have had your guts for garters if he found out.'

'Yeah, tell me about it,' Scott agreed. 'That whole experience was what inspired me to specialise in virus removal.'

Taking another slug of his drink Ross spoke again. 'I used to give out pirated copies of Windows XP. Every member of my extended family and all my friends got one. Then they re-pirated it to their friends and so on. I reckon I cost Microsoft thousands of bucks.'

They all gave mock expressions of horror.

'I put laxatives in Mr Small's coffee one day,' Bev said

quietly.

'Whoa!' exclaimed Rosie. 'Bev wins hands down!' Looking at her workmate expectantly she said, 'Come on, you can't give us that without the rest of the details.'

Bev blushed. 'When we changed to the new accounts system he was just unbearable. He blamed me every time something went wrong and refused to accept responsibility for the fact that he was the one who wanted it in the first place.'

'He's not always the most reasonable man,' Rosie said.

'Anyway,' Bev said, 'one day I couldn't take it anymore. So I laced his International Roast with *Go-Lax* and he suddenly had more urgent business to attend to.'

They were still laughing about it when Nicky came over to clear their table.

By the time ninety minutes ticked over the gang of four had become so comfortable in each other's company that none of them wanted to leave. Eventually though, they knew they should get back.

'I want to finish early so I can gear up for a *huge* night,' Rosie explained.

'Here, here,' Ross agreed.

Leaving her phone on the table Rosie went up to settle the bill while the others continued to talk. A loud techno ring tone startled them all when the mobile rang. Bev grabbed the phone but she wasn't wearing her glasses and accidentally hit the loudspeaker key. Holding it at arm's length and peering at the newfangled touch screen, she still hadn't worked it out by the time it switched to message

111

bank still on loudspeaker.

'Hey Rosie, it's Kath. I'm hearing you, I'm hearing you – New Year's Eve can be a real drag and it's hard to keep up the pretence of being the real party animal. Maybe you could just stay home and tell everyone you were with someone else? That's the great thing about being a cop; I am pretty much guaranteed to be working, so it's not even something I have to contemplate. Anyway, I just wanted to say that I hope you find something to do. Talk soon, Bye.'

The three workmates looked at each other and then over at Rosie, who had heard the whole thing from her place in the queue for the till.

When she returned to the table at first Rosie tried to look unconcerned, but seeing the way the others were looking at her with such pity she decided to come clean.

As a single thirty-something and the last one standing from her circle of friends she had recently found herself in a social wasteland. Sure her married/partnered friends invited her to things, but those events were always full of other couples. She had lived the dinner party scene from *Bridget Jones' Diary* too many times to mention. Besides, most of them had kids now as well, so any socialising had to be booked weeks in advance and be over by nine o'clock.

Her younger friends from work and from her netball team were the other extreme. No weekend was complete for them without getting completely written off on both Friday and Saturday nights and sleeping all day Sunday. Rosie had been there and done that in great style, but as much as she had initially hated to admit it she was now well and truly over the nightclub scene.

After explaining this she said, 'It's okay, you don't all have to look at me like that. Let's just admit it, my social life these days is a work of fiction and apart from a few half-hearted pity invites, tonight I really have nowhere to go. I wish I didn't mind like you Bev, or that I had a spouse like you Scott or that I was a drinker like you Ross, but the truth is I do mind. I feel like a failure.'

'Oh Rosie no you're not, or if you are then I am too,' Bev said as she clasped Rosie's hand, and then told the group how she really felt about staying home.

Scott raised his hand. 'I'll out myself as well. I'm not at all happy with the idea of staying home alone just because Lara is working.'

Ross looked at his shoes for a while before mumbling that his night was going to be far from a happy alcohol fuelled celebration.

None of them spoke as they walked back to work. They ignored the band that was setting up in readiness for the street party and paid little attention to the Happy New Year banner that was being strung across the main street.

Scott made the suggestion tentatively at first.

While Lara had made it clear she didn't want him to go out and have fun, she hadn't said anything about not having work mates over for a bit of a catch up.

Ross was doubtful. 'Sounds like you're on a bit of a sticky wicket there mate.'

'Well, it would have to be a quiet-ish kind of night,' Scott said. 'If we have a big rowdy celebration the neighbours would be sure to mention it.'

'Quiet-ish would be just fine with me,' Rosie said.

Thrilled at the thought of her first New Year's Eve out of the house in almost thirty years, Bev couldn't have been more excited if she was planning to be on the foreshore of Sydney Harbour watching the fireworks. 'I could whip up some party food if everyone wants to contribute something to the kitty.'

Rosie offered to make some punch and bring over *Balderdash* which was great fun.

The only one who hadn't committed was Ross.

'It might be a bit of a comedown for you mate, compared to the stuff you usually end up doing,' Scott said.

Ross sighed wearily.

'It would be nice if you could come,' Bev said.

'Well it does sound like an all right kind of shindig,' Ross agreed.

Scott informed Ross there could be no question of him staying over, that he would either have to limit his drinking to stay under the limit, or he would have to sleep in his car at least one street away as there was no chance he would get a taxi.

Ross agreed that either option would work.

There was a much higher energy level at SmallWorld that afternoon. The evening, which to each of them, albeit privately, had previously seemed to stretch out ad infinitum now had a shape to it. They had somewhere to go, and people with whom to celebrate the transition to the new year.

Bev and Rosie cleaned out the storeroom and completed the stationary order, a job which had been shelved for the past two months. They chatted easily as they worked and wondered why the task had been repeatedly put off for so long. Starting the New Year with a clean storeroom was a nice feeling.

The back corner of the workshop was a graveyard of assorted junk that nobody knew what to do with. As Scott rearranged the shelves so that each held various useable parts, placed a large box labelled 'For The Tip' near the door and cleared the bench space so it could be used, he kicked himself for not doing it sooner.

Meanwhile, Ross finished the tweaks to the new email system that Mr Small had been reminding him about for the last six weeks. He had to admit that it would save everybody time, now that there was a proper filter for inter-office messages. As rigid and unbending as Mr Small could be, the guy did have some good ideas.

After a call to Mr Small to reassure him that everything was shipshape in the office, Rosie gave everybody an early mark at 4.30. The day that had started with so little enthusiasm finished on a much higher note. Scott gave them directions to his house and they all waved each other goodbye as Rosie locked the door. As they headed to their cars each one of them looked forward to the evening ahead.

New Years Eve didn't seem so bad after all.

• • • • •

'That was an appropriate choice for today, considering what we were just talking about,' Grace said, as she closed the book and put it down.

Edith blinked.

'I really related to it,' Grace admitted. 'I hate New Year's Eve and I thought I was the only one who did. But going by this story, maybe I'm not alone with that.'

Edith raised an eyebrow. Although unsure if she was agreeing or disagreeing with her, Grace had learned enough about her new friend to know that she wanted her to elaborate further.

'There's a lot of pressure to celebrate on New Year's Eve,' Grace said. 'Some years that can be a good thing. Like when you're a kid a whole new year seems really exciting, but when you get older it can just remind you of what you haven't managed to achieve in the previous year.'

This time Edith eyed Grace in such a way that it was impossible not to interpret what she was thinking. 'Yeah I know twenty is still pretty young. But sometimes I feel really old.'

Grace had certainly not intended that statement to be anything other than an honest appraisal of her own life. But catching a glimpse of Edith's stricken face she realised she had touched on something a lot deeper. She didn't know if the other woman was expressing sadness about her own life or about the fact Grace was so powerless to do anything good with her own. All Grace knew was that despite her reserve and stunted emotional wellbeing, she could not sit and watch a widowed stroke victim in a nursing home sit and cry without offering her a little comfort.

Hugging is such an instinctive human act, Grace

realised as she held Edith's frail body as it trembled with grief. She couldn't remember the last time she had hugged anybody, but apparently it was like riding a bike, you never lost the knack. No words were spoken, really what could she say that would make Edith's circumstances any better? But she knew that was not what Edith was seeking.

The moment eventually passed – as they always do – and Grace moved back to her chair and back to other elements of the story.

As she bid Edith goodbye Grace wasn't sure how to feel. Although the other woman was recomposed and apparently back to normal, a deep melancholy continued to emanate from her. Wasn't that fair enough though? Even upbeat people had bad days sometimes.

They were like two unconnected pieces of the same puzzle – Edith who had the right attitude and the confidence to live a normal life but was held back by a broken body and Grace who could physically go anywhere she wanted to go but was trapped by the confines of her mind.

Seeing gnome man coming down the hall towards her Grace made an effort to smile as he passed. But this time he zoomed right by without so much as glancing at her. Grace sighed wearily; obviously she was giving off some pretty sad vibes today. Putting her head down she hurried to the exit, determined not to infect anybody else.

* * * * *

The New Year's Eve after her high school graduation was

supposed to be the most amazing of Grace's life. Her birthday was on New Year's Day and she loved the fact that she could ride the coattails of the party night of the year to ensure her eighteenth birthday was celebrated in style. She and her friends back home had started planning the party back in Year Eleven.

Of course things were different when she went away to Strauss, but plans for the big night had remained fixed. Her best friend Alex emailed regularly with updates on the playlist or the menu and kept track of the financial contribution they were all making to the event. Renting the penthouse at Q1 in Surfers Paradise had not come cheap, but divided amongst ten they all agreed it was worth the investment.

Grace never found out if the others had gone ahead with the big party. Of course it wouldn't have been her birthday party anymore, but it was still New Year's Eve and it would have been fun to host a big celebration there anyway. By then she had changed her mobile number and closed her old email address and Facebook account to prevent any contact. She assumed they were so mad at her anyway that they probably did go ahead just to spite her.

If there was one thing the past few years had taught her, it was that familiarity meant safety. After four visits, Rosehill Gardens had become familiar to Grace, comfortable even. Leaving the haven of her car and walking to the front door felt safe now. Greeting people as she walked along the hallways towards Edith's room could still be confronting, but only if it was somebody she didn't know. And even then generally it was fine. They all smiled, they were just grateful she volunteered her time to spend with Edith. Grace was just another face, another person who shared a little of the load and helped make their days at Rosehill a bit easier.

Her pulse increased a little as she approached the nurses' station. It was one thing to say hello when you walked past someone in the hall, but it was still easier if she could just slink past unseen. But then again they had a closed circuit TV monitor on their desk so she would be in their line of vision. It would probably seem very rude not to say something.

She may have stood there all morning dithering if Janice – one of Edith's nurses – hadn't looked up. 'Hi Grace. I guess it must be Tuesday if you're here?' she said with a smile.

'You said it,' she replied with a return smile, before resuming her journey to the east wing. Doubt plagued her mind for a moment. Was 'you said it' the appropriate response? On the spur of the moment it had seemed like a quick, clever remark but now it seemed odd and awkward. Hesitating a second she turned back, frantically trying to come up with something else. But Janice was already engrossed in her paperwork again. Grace relaxed.

So used to seeing Edith ready and waiting for her, Grace was shocked to enter the room and see two nurses tending to Edith, who was lying flat on her back on the bed. Marion was also there, dusting around the window frame.

'Oh, I'm so sorry, I didn't mean to intrude … I'll leave,' she mumbled, hastily attempting to back out of the door.

'No, Grace wait,' Marion called. 'It's okay, they're almost finished.'

'Are you sure?'

'Yes it's fine,' one of the nurses assured her as she adjusted the nasal prongs and moved the portable oxygen tank back against the wall. The tall and big boned nurse was familiar but Grace couldn't read her name tag.

Grace hung back near the door until the nurses were finished then approached cautiously. It was strange to see Edith wearing just a normal nursing home gown with her hair in a simple plait and her face devoid of makeup. The nurses had raised the top end of her bed a little, but she was much lower down than normal and Grace felt too tall and imposing as she stood near the bed.

'You'd better sit down Grace,' Marion said, 'you'd be a bit overwhelming from that angle.'

Needing no further prompting, Grace sank down into the armchair and tried not to look too closely at Edith.

'She's all right,' Marion reassured. 'Just a chest infection. It's part and parcel of being bed ridden.'

'That sucks.'

Marion let out a peal of laughter that ended with a snort. 'Indeed it does!' she gasped. 'Well said hon, I've never heard you use an expression like that before.'

'Well, I don't usually…' Grace began.

'Grace stop apologising! I wasn't criticising you, just stating a fact. I like that you said it – you are right, it does suck. Please don't feel you need to censor what you want to say around Edith. She likes people to be up front, don't you lovie?'

Edith blinked, somewhat tiredly Grace thought.

'All right,' Grace said. 'Do you think they still want me to read today if Edith isn't well? I can make another time if you want.'

'No, don't go. All this morning while Edith here has been turned and jabbed and had her back pounded so she didn't choke on her own phlegm she was looking forward to your visit.'

Grace wondered just how the cleaner knew this but didn't like to disagree.

'Trust me Grace, she loves having you come to visit.'

'I like it too,' Grace replied, her voice catching a little. How was it that she, Grace, who was so insignificant in the outside world had come to mean so much to another person? She was glad Edith couldn't see her eyes misting over as she leaned down and hauled out the book, ready to embark on the next chapter.

Audrey was surprised by how calmly the idea of suicide came to her. It wasn't in the midst of a horrible anxiety attack or a crippling bout of depression; it just slipped into her mind one day as she sat in her favourite armchair listening to the clock tick in the oppressive silence of her house.

Never had she entertained such a thought before.

Starting life as sickly baby who had battled the odds to survive her first couple of years and then as a frail teenager and adult, Audrey's fighting spirit had always carried her through.

But now all she felt was an aching loneliness.

Looking at the photograph of Martin on the coffee table, Audrey still couldn't believe the cruelty of it. Strong robust Martin had cared for Audrey throughout their marriage and had even passed up his own interests and dreams to keep her comfortable and as healthy as possible. It was Martin who had held her hand before the risky, experimental heart surgery that had unexpectedly transformed Audrey's life at the age of fifty-eight.

Just when she had been given the opportunity to repay his dedication by being able to travel and go hiking with him as they had always dreamed, he had been struck down by a rare terminal lung condition and within a few short months he was dead. Now a year since his passing, Audrey missed him more every day, rather than less. Those who said time healed all wounds didn't have a clue.

The thought percolated in Audrey's mind over the following week. It would be easy enough to do. She still had a cupboard full of her old heart medication, an overdose could be taken quietly and she could just drift off one night.

Yet something held her back.

Repeatedly, she asked herself why she just didn't get it over with as she ate breakfast, lunch and dinner alone in her quiet kitchen, in her spotless house. There were no children to be upset by her passing, nor did she have siblings of her own.

But there was always a reason to not do it just yet. She hadn't yet cleaned out the spare room, she hadn't finished the photo albums and her garden wasn't quite in bloom yet – it wouldn't do to leave it in the in between stage.

Besides she didn't want Martin's family or her elderly aunt and cousins to have to sort through a mess. Nor did she like the idea of being one of those poor people found weeks or months after their death, because nobody noticed they were missing.

Having dithered for weeks, Audrey made her decision one lonely Monday morning as another endless day stretched out in front of her. Right, she decided, I'm going to get the garden in shape and put my affairs in order.

Checking her calendar she noted Dr James was due for a home visit in three weeks on Monday the 25th. A cheerful, practical, middle-aged woman, Dr James was used to dealing with death and wouldn't be too traumatised to find Audrey dead in her bed. I'll just make sure I hide all the evidence, Audrey decided. It will just look like I passed away peacefully in my sleep.

Much more settled now that she had made up her mind, Audrey compiled her to-do list, surprised how many items were on there but confident she could get through them in the time she had left. It was ironic, really, that now she was planning to die she had more motivation than she'd had all year.

Upon collecting her mail the next day, Audrey found two

pamphlets nestled between her phone bill and bank statement. She sighed in annoyance, couldn't those people read? What was the point of having a "no junk mail" sticker if nobody took it seriously?

Audrey couldn't explain what made her read the fluorescent green slip of paper, rather than dumping it straight in the recycling bin with the other white one.

Do you feel lonely or empty? Don't despair! There are always options available – any problem can be overcome. Please call Careline Counselling any time. We're here to help.

Stunned, Audrey stared at the piece of paper for a moment before slipping it in her pocket. Was this Martin's doing? Had he somehow arranged things to guide her out of this pit she had fallen into? She knew how disappointed he would be if she threw in the towel now, just when she had the chance to live a bit.

'Oh, Martin,' Audrey murmured as she weeded her pansy bed that afternoon. 'It's just so awful here by myself. I'd really just rather come and join you.'

Sitting down in her armchair after dinner, Audrey fiddled with the pamphlet, curling and uncurling the edges. How could some stranger possibly help her? Nobody else could begin to understand just how devastating her loss was, could they?

Glancing at Martin's photo she sighed then picked up the phone and dialled.

The voice that answered was warm and compassionate. 'Hello Careline Counselling, my name is Olivia and I'm here to help.'

Audrey paused, debating whether to say something or just hang up. Her problems seemed insignificant compared to what other people went through. Maybe this was just for really desperate cases and she shouldn't be wasting their time.

Her finger was hovering, ready to disconnect when Olivia's voice came through again. 'Please speak to me. You've come this far, just tell me what's on your mind.'

'Well, I … uh …' To Audrey's surprise she began to sob. 'I'm s-s-sorry—'

'Don't be sorry, let the tears out. I can wait as long as you need me to.'

With Olivia's gentle prompting Audrey eventually told her story and her recent decision that the world wouldn't miss her if she went.

'Oh Audrey, of course that's not true. You're just a bit hidden away at the moment. Once we get you back out there you'll feel differently.'

'Well I don't know…' Audrey replied. 'There just doesn't seem much point.'

'Can you promise me six weeks? Can you stick around that long?'

'I don't know Olivia, I just can't imagine ever feeling happy again. Why wait?'

'Well, it's just about summer, the nicest time of year. Think about all those nice long evenings and beautiful sunrises. Not to mention the cricket and the tennis.'

'Oh yes, I've always been a sports fan. Martin used to play cricket every Saturday, down in the park here.'

'There you go! Please Audrey, do it for me? I've just connected with you tonight and I'd miss you if you went.' Olivia's voice was full of life.

The kind words made Audrey teary again. 'I suppose I could.'

'Of course you can. Now, I know this is anonymous so I can't ask your address, but if I give you a delivery code you can go to your local post office and pick up a little parcel I'll send.'

'What kind of parcel? I'm really not sure…'

'I've been doing this work a long time Audrey and over the years I've put together a bit of a program designed to help people find themselves again. It's nothing that's ever been published or proven, but over the years people have told me it has helped them. Will you please look at it if I send it out to you?'

Despite herself Audrey's curiosity was piqued. 'Yes I promise.'

'That's the spirit. Now where is your closest post office?'

Audrey couldn't help but feel a sense of anticipation as she ate breakfast two days later. She hadn't been anywhere except the supermarket for weeks. Since her neighbour Joan had moved to Melbourne to live with her daughter and two other couples she'd been friends with had sold up to the developer who was building townhouses on their house lots, life in Audrey's street was very quiet. There were no more coffee mornings, and no more sharing lifts to the Sunny Seniors group she and Martin had been part of. Having never learnt to drive Audrey didn't like to be a burden to anyone and ask them to take her.

It was only a short walk to the post office and despite her apathy Audrey was entranced by the beautiful late spring day. The azure sky and balmy breeze were like a tonic to her weary spirit. It wasn't busy in the post office and the young woman who served her seemed happy to chat as she located the small parcel and handed it to Audrey.

'Parcels are such fun aren't they? There's always the delicious hope that there might be something exciting inside.'

'Yes, you're so right,' Audrey agreed. 'I have the feeling this one might be quite exciting indeed.'

Audrey examined the thick yellow A4 envelope when she got home. Although the return address had been blacked out with permanent marker, holding it up to the light Audrey could still read that it came from South East University, which was just a few streets away. That gave her some confidence. If the counselling service was run by the university then the people they had working there must be qualified in some way.

Opening the envelope, she found a series of smaller envelopes and an accompanying letter which read:

Open a new envelope at the beginning of each week. Open them in order, don't skip ahead and read them all to start with. It works best if you just follow the instructions.

Keen to get started on the program Audrey ripped open the first envelope. The small piece of paper read:

Even if you find the days long and have nothing to fill them, don't succumb to sleeping your time away. Set the alarm, get up and make your bed (to avoid the temptation to get back in), shower and dress yourself like you have somewhere to go and something to do even if you don't.

The sting of disappointment hit Audrey when she finished reading. She turned the page over and looked inside the small envelope to see if she had missed something. But there was nothing else.

Audrey sighed wearily. She already did these things every day. Always awake by six o'clock without any need for an alarm, Audrey's bed was made within minutes of her getting out of it. And she never sat down to breakfast without having her shower and getting dressed. It was a habit her mother had drummed into her.

Swallowing back tears Audrey sat down in her armchair and stared up at the ceiling. Why had she let herself get excited about something? It was always so hard to live with the disappointment afterwards.

Picking up a gardening magazine, Audrey flipped through it listlessly before examining the large envelope again. It had said not to read through all the instructions without completing the previous assignment. It hadn't said you couldn't skip ahead if you already did what it suggested.

A small frisson of energy surged as Audrey picked up envelope #2. Inside was another small piece of paper that read:

> *Your task this week is to do at least one anonymous kind deed each day. There is no limit on how small or extravagant the deed can be – just do what you are able to.*

Filled with purpose, Audrey got up off the recliner and went into the kitchen for a pen and paper. Sitting down at the table she began to write a list.

Given that she was up and organised so early each day, Audrey found herself getting impatient when she had to wait around for several hours before she could undertake her kind deed for the day.

On Monday she baked a casserole and some scones for the harassed looking single mother across the street. Although the food was packed and ready to deliver by half past nine, Audrey had to wait until almost noon before the woman left the house. Feeling like a criminal and sure she looked very suspicious, Audrey managed to drop the items on the front door step without being seen.

On Tuesday she took the washing off the line and ironed it for the young bachelor who lived next door. They had a nodding acquaintance and he had mentioned once how he often left his washing on the line for days and never got around to ironing it until the last minute. She had planned to fetch it as soon as he left for work, but a quick shower of rain meant she had to wait two hours for it to get dry.

On Wednesday she bought a stack of current magazines and slipped them in the mailbox of the student share house at the end of the street.

On Thursday she paid a taxi driver to deliver a box of handmade chocolates to Martin's niece Amelia, who had always been very kind to her.

On Friday she went into the busy café three streets away, chose table number fourteen at random and went up to the counter and paid for their morning tea.

Over the weekend she wrote donation cheques for three charities then spent the afternoons tidying the garden beds around the tiny community hall up near the shopping centre.

• • • • •

Although there was technically no reason why she couldn't open the next envelope before the appointed day, Audrey chose to wait and do things by the book.

The next note was written on the same lined paper and was similarly short and to the point. Her task for the following week was to finish two uncompleted household projects. Audrey immediately started sorting out her photo albums and as she worked contentedly while listening to talkback radio, she wondered why it had taken the words of a virtual stranger to give her the motivation to do something she could have done anytime over the past six months.

She mentioned it to Olivia that evening. Audrey had fallen into the habit of ringing her every second night, just to check in.

'You know Audrey, you can only do your best with what's in front of you. When you're grieving, you just don't think the same way. Life loses all its colour. Isn't it great that you're feeling enough like your old self to want to get the albums finished?'

'Yes, I suppose,' Audrey agreed. 'But now I'm wondering why I'm bothering. Who will ever see them? I felt so good today, but now, well I'm…' she sighed uncertainly.

'Now, now Audrey. Remember, we talked about how the evenings are the worst? Don't undo all the good by getting maudlin. Have a Tim Tam and find something funny to watch on TV. Didn't you tell me you're a huge *Fawlty Towers* fan?'

'Yes, I think it's my all-time favourite show.'

'Right, it's on in fifteen minutes. Promise me you'll watch it and laugh yourself silly.'

'All right, I will.'

Her second task was doing up the spare room. She and Martin had rarely had people to stay, but she had always like the idea of a proper guest room. I could get some new curtains, she thought, and a new bedspread. It's such a lovely, sunny room and it looks right into the garden. Full of

131

enthusiasm, she headed to the bus stop.

• • • • •

Eager to open the next envelope and discover its contents, Audrey made a little celebration of it. Preparing a cup of tea in her best china and a slice of the decadent carrot cake she had treated herself to at the bakery, she made herself comfortable in her recliner before ceremonially slitting the envelope open. Taking the single sheet of paper, her heart lurched when she read the short paragraph.

> *Have a five minute conversation with somebody every day (not including yours truly). It must go beyond the basic pleasantries. Engage the other person and take a genuine interest in what they are saying.*

Audrey wasn't sure how to go about meeting new people. She felt she was at an age where it was difficult to make friends. Everyone was already in their little cliques and probably weren't interested in letting an outsider in. A genuinely shy person at heart, Audrey had always been content to let Martin do the talking when they met someone new. Maybe I'll just have to skip this step she decided.

When she mentioned it that night, Olivia was surprisingly stern about not cheating the system.

'Now come on Audrey, can you imagine what a dull old life it would be if there was an age limit on making new friends? Besides the instruction is not to make a new best friend, it is just to engage in pleasant conversation.'

'I really wouldn't know where to begin.'

'Right, go to the library tomorrow and ask them about their computer classes.'

'But I have no interest in learning about computers.'

'There you go again Audrey, reading more into the instruction than you need to. I didn't say you had to DO the classes, just ask about them.'

'But I know nothing about computers. Won't it seem put upon?'

'Not if you're asking about the classes because you want to learn. Admit you're a complete novice, it will make for a much more interesting conversation.'

Audrey was quickly learning that it was easier to do what Olivia suggested rather than argue the point. 'Okay, okay I'll do it.'

After a tentative start, Audrey embraced the conversation challenge. The young woman in the post office became a favourite, as did the long-winded man in the corner shop. All Audrey had to do was mention the weather (the climate is changing, you mark my words!), the recent rise in council rates (daylight robbery!) or the youth of today (louts, the lot of them!) and she was guaranteed at least a ten minute exchange.

She supposed she shouldn't have been surprised when Olivia upped the ante mid challenge. 'That's the way Audrey, I'm so pleased to hear that conversation has become a daily habit. But I think you're getting a bit comfortable with your regulars, so as well as talking to them you need to add a new person each day.'

'Oh Olivia, I really don't think...'

'Audrey...' Olivia began.

'Fine,' Audrey said.

Although initially relieved when the conversation challenge was over, Audrey was also a little disappointed. Once she pushed herself out of her comfort zone, she had come to enjoy the daily exchanges. It only occurred to her on the last day that she could continue the practice and, of course, that was obviously Olivia's plan in the first place.

• • • • •

So eager to discover what the next envelope contained, Audrey was awake at 4.30 am on the following Monday. Snapping on her bedside light she donned her reading glasses and slid the envelope open with the emery board she kept near her bed. The first thing she noticed was the size of the page, it was A4 rather than the small, notebook sized ones she had become used to. The second thing was the Woolworths Gift Card taped to the outside of the paper. Intrigued, Audrey unfolded the note and read the text, her eyes widening as she did so.

Welcome to Audrey's restaurant! When was the last time you treated yourself to your favourite meal? How often do you just go for the easy option of beans on toast just because it's too much trouble to cook for one? Your challenge this week is to treat every evening meal like a fine dining experience. Prepare a menu, buy your ingredients and celebrate your food every night. Include dessert if you like! Please use the enclosed Woolworths Gift Card to offset the extra costs.

As an extra challenge you can deliver an extra portion of each favourite meal to the City Homeless Shelter the following morning. Ring them for instructions.

Shaking her head Audrey chuckled. She didn't know where Olivia got her ideas, but she had certainly hit the nail on the head. Cooking had been one of the few activities that Audrey was capable of when she was ill and for her it had truly been one of life's great pleasures. It was also one of the few things she had been able to do for Martin. Yet she hadn't cooked anything more imaginative than meat and three veg for the past year. Reaching for the pen on her bedside table she turned the piece of paper over and starting writing.

Normally reserved and softly spoken, Audrey couldn't contain the excitement in her voice when she spoke to Olivia a few nights later. 'The homeless shelter are so thrilled to get my meals,' she said enthusiastically. 'I had no idea one small gesture could mean so much. Besides it's so much nicer to cook for somebody besides yourself. They've asked me to volunteer in the kitchen a couple of times a week.'

'And will you?' Olivia asked.

'Well, yes I think I will,' Audrey replied.

'So, does that mean you're going to stick around?'

'Yes Olivia, I think I might.'

* * * * *

Unlike the previous weeks where she had rushed to tear open that weeks' envelope, Audrey was reluctant to open the final one. Sipping her tea at the kitchen table, she turned the envelope over in her hands, pondering why she just didn't rip it open. I don't want it to end, Audrey realised. These envelopes and the tasks within have made such a difference to my life and I hate the idea of going back to the way I was.

Setting the final instruction aside, she went outside to work on her garden. All those years she was ill, Audrey had been the gardening director while Martin had done all the physical labour. She had often apologised to him for having to work so hard while she sat and watched, but he had always assured her it was good honest labour. Now since she was able to do the work herself she realised he was right. There was something almost primal about having your hands in the soil as well as pruning and weeding. Even the simple act of watering the flowers was a pleasure, especially on a beautiful morning like today.

Audrey noticed the teenage girl as she turned into the street. Tall and willowy, she had the kind of figure many women would kill for. Dressed in a denim skirt and a white singlet, she wore bright pink thongs on her feet and was carrying a book satchel. She must be a student, Audrey realised. Her street used to be a bit of a thoroughfare to the nearby university, as there was a bus stop right on the corner and the budget conscious students knew it was almost a dollar cheaper to get off two stops early and walk the last kilometre. But then the council had changed the zones, so it was only worthwhile to get off early for those coming a fair distance.

The girl seemed to be in no hurry as she meandered along the street. Up close Audrey noticed how attractive she was, with an almost porcelain complexion and curly blonde hair hanging loosely around her shoulders. Yet her face was sad and her demeanour troubled. I wonder what a young girl with her whole life in front of her has to feel sad about? Audrey pondered as she uncoiled the hose a little further and moved to her front garden bed.

A few weeks earlier Audrey would have kept her head down, terrified of making eye contact with a stranger, but today she remembered her conversation challenge and spoke before she had a chance to talk herself out of it. 'Good morning,' she ventured, her heart beating a little faster with the realisation she had taken an important step all by herself.

'Hello,' the girl answered sadly, stopping near the front gate.

Audrey was a little shocked. A brief greeting as someone walked past was one thing, but having them stop and chat was another. It's all right Audrey, she told herself

137

calmly. Remember the rules of basic conversation. 'Lovely day isn't it?' she said with a shy smile.

'Yes it is,' the girl agreed.

What have I got to chat to a teenager about? Maybe I could ask her about uni, but then I don't know anything about the uni, even though I've lived close to it for thirty years.

'You have such a lovely garden,' the girl said, breaking the impasse.

'Thank you. I do what I can with it.'

'It's the best in the street and it always cheers me up when I'm feeling a bit down. You can't feel too sad when there's a sea of pink and white roses to look at.'

'I can't imagine a lovely young lady like yourself could have too much to feel sad about,' Audrey said shyly.

The girl sighed heavily. 'I've just found out I'll have to give up uni for a while and I'm so disappointed. I'm studying teaching and I can't wait to get qualified and start my career.'

Despite herself Audrey was intrigued. 'Why do you have to give up?' she asked.

'Well, I live over in Cloverdale. You know where that is right?'

'Yes, it's over the other side of the range, lovely country out there.'

'Uh huh. I catch the bus in every day because I just can't afford the cost of accommodation. But now they've cancelled the daily bus service and I don't have a car. I guess I'll have to work a year or two and save up.'

'That seems like a real shame, when you're so keen.

You don't know anyone you could board with?'

'No, unfortunately. It would be great if I did, boarding is way cheaper than paying rent on a place and I wouldn't have to pay for weekends or anything when I'm back at home. My parents have a farm and they need me to help out.'

'Does the uni have an accommodation service that could help you find somewhere?'

'Well yeah, they do, but there's a major shortage of boarding accommodation. Nobody seems to want to do it anymore.'

'Right,' Audrey murmured.

'Oh well, it will all work out somehow,' the girl said with false cheerfulness. 'By the way, I'm Melanie.'

'Very pleased to meet you Melanie, I'm Audrey.'

'Have a nice day in your lovely garden, Audrey.'

'Yes, I will,' Audrey said distractedly, waving the young woman off.

She couldn't, of course. Now Audrey couldn't stop thinking about Melanie as she pruned her rosebushes and spread mulch around her impatiens. Having had to give up so many of her own dreams due to her illness, she knew how devastating it could be. It just didn't seem right that Melanie would have to delay her education because of financial constraints.

• • • • •

Six months later, Audrey couldn't believe that she'd ever had time to feel lonely. Between volunteering at the homeless shelter and organising meals for herself and Melanie, she barely had time to catch her favourite TV shows in the afternoon. Later that fateful day she had met Melanie, she had finally opened the remaining envelope. It had told her to take a risk and do something challenging.

It had been surprisingly easy to track Melanie down through the university and offer her bed and board in her home. She'd had to go through the accommodation selection process, but it had all been a formality. Audrey's life had been transformed from empty to overflowing and despite still missing Martin desperately, she now possessed an enthusiasm for life she couldn't quite believe herself.

She still rang Olivia once a week to let her know how she was getting on, ending every call with a passionate thank you for transforming her life.

'No Audrey, I just gave you the tools, you did the transforming yourself,' Olivia always assured her.

• • • • •

Olivia smiled contentedly as she hung the phone up, glad of her ability to think outside the square. It was just as well she used a separate phone for each service she offered or she would never be able to keep track!

Universities could be very bureaucratic places and nowhere more so than the accommodation office she had worked in for the past decade. When they couldn't come up with a feasible plan to tackle the affordable accommodation shortage, she had taken matters into her own hands.

Identifying several key streets within walking distance of the campus Olivia discovered there were lots of big houses with many empty rooms. Thinking strategically she had done her letterbox drop, offering either financial advice for those wanting to top up their income or counselling for those who were lonely. Anticipating a response rate of around ten percent, Olivia was amazed when almost half the homeowners responded in some fashion.

For the cost of a bit of her time to talk to people on the phone, Olivia had managed to secure accommodation for thirty five students and had improved the psychological and financial wellbeing of twenty-four homeowners. This number would only increase as she expanded to another cluster of suburbs with easy access to the new improved uni bus service. Along the way she had also made many new friends, even though they would never meet face to face. The wonderful conversations she continued to share with people like Audrey were the unexpected bonus of the whole scheme.

It was win-win all round and nobody ever needed to know the full story.

• • • • •

'Gosh, that had a darker theme,' Marion remarked as she mopped around the bed.

'Yeah, it did,' said Grace quietly.

Before she could say anything more Edith succumbed to another violent coughing fit, the sound of each cough a truly terrifying thing.

Grace snapped to an upright position in the saggy chair,

wanting to help yet frozen with fear. 'Can I...? Do you...?' she stammered, her eyes darting frantically around for the call button.

Marion shook her head and held Edith's hand as the woman's body continued to convulse.

Fighting the panic rising in her own body, Grace asked, 'Are you sure?'

Again Marion nodded, more deliberately this time as the coughing gradually slowed. 'She's fine. It really does sound worse than it is because her body is so frail. But you're okay now aren't you lovie?'

Edith managed a very weary blink.

Grace sat quietly and tried not to stare as Edith's breathing gradually returned to normal and her complexion retreated from bright red back to her normal, albeit pale shade.

'Um, do you want me to keep going?' Grace asked nervously, hoping there would be no more coughing.

'Yes, off you go Grace. I'd like to hear what you thought of the story and I'm sure Edith would too,' said Marion.

'Uh, well it was a bit darker, like you said – I mean suicide isn't a normal theme for a short story.'

'That's true.'

'I can kind of understand how she felt,' Grace admitted quietly. Although her eyes were downcast when she said it, Grace could feel Marion's intense gaze upon her.

'Why?'

Still avoiding Marion's eyes, Grace shrugged. 'Sometimes everything just gets too hard and you can't see a way out. Audrey was so lonely and so isolated she just couldn't imagine any other life for herself.'

'Do you have many friends Grace?'

Grace shook her head silently.

'Family?'

It was only a micro pause, but Marion noticed it before Grace shook her head again.

'You live by yourself, right?'

Grace nodded.

'You wouldn't ever…?'

'No I wouldn't, honestly. I'm not saying I'm thinking of suicide, I just mean I understand how circumstances can lead people there.'

'You're sure?'

Grace nodded. 'I promise.'

Marion straightened Edith's wedding photo before turning back to Grace. 'The great thing about this story is that it shows how life can flip on you all of a sudden. You just have to do one little thing and suddenly everything changes. For Audrey it was a phone call, a fifteen minute conversation that set her on a whole new path. The world is full of choices Grace, you just have to have enough courage to make them.'

Grace nodded wearily. Everyone spoke about courage like it was so easy to come by. She was all out of courage. More than ready to change the subject she glanced down at the book again. 'Uh lets move onto the other story elements before my time runs out.'

Edith managed a tiny nod.

It always amazed Grace how suddenly the symptoms could appear. Just as she was wrapping up her final thoughts on the story her heart began to beat so loud and fast she was sure Edith and Marion must be able to hear it. Then heat suffused her whole body as if the air conditioning had suddenly been turned up to forty degrees. She could feel the walls closing in on her and the roof caving. Her mind whirled as she tried to cope with not only the onset of the panic attack but what she would say to Marion to allow her to escape.

Today luck was on her side. Before the others seemed to notice her discomfiture a nurse bustled in and informed Edith that the doctor was ready to see her. Grateful beyond measure Grace managed to get up and bow out of the room without any further ado. Looking straight ahead she made her way through the centre and to the car park. Fumbling with her car key she finally managed to open the door and collapse inside. Crawling into the backseat she curled into the foetal position, closed her eyes and let the tears flow.

* * * * *

It was weird how the panic attacks didn't actually start until after the event. While she had felt stress and uncertainty after she left Strauss, Grace had never experienced the overwhelming sensation that the world was about to end. Having no real knowledge of panic attacks, in that moment of her first episode she had truly believed she was about to die.

The panic attacks were the tipping point for Grace. Before that she'd had some hope she might sort things out and had believed that getting back on her original life path was a possibility. But once she realised that a force that strong could appear from nowhere and reduce her to a cowering shell, it was time to face reality.

Applying for a disability pension had been difficult at first but Grace knew it was her lifeline. Her social worker had been blunt but helpful and once the decision was made the forms were lodged within hours. She knew she was lucky to be accepted so easily when so many other deserving people had to fight for the same right.

Grace didn't like admitting she was wrong, especially to herself. She had been dragged into the Rejoin Program knowing for absolute certain that it would not help her. Yet six weeks in even she couldn't ignore the positive results. Doing something constructive, rather than just hiding away from the world *was* helpful. It gave her purpose and something to look forward to. It gave her Tuesday and her week some structure. It had even built up her confidence a bit. On her first visit she could never have imagined that she would be able to walk easily through the front door without anxiety, or greet staff with an easy smile, or that she could actually feel part of the running of Rosehill Gardens.

Grace walked normally now, rather than timidly clinging to the edges of the corridors. She held her head – if not high – at least at an appropriate level so she could see where she was going. Along the way she greeted staff members without feeling too self-conscious that she might say the wrong thing or they would think badly of her for any real or imagined reason.

One thing she did still struggle with, however, was the sight of Sylvia. Despite the other woman's courteous and professional manner, she was still the keeper of Grace's secrets and was the one person at Rosehill with the power to alter Grace's future should she so choose to do so. Even a glimpse of Sylvia in the distance was enough to send Grace scurrying back into the shadows or to lurk in the nearest public bathroom until enough time had passed for her to have moved on to where she was going.

Caught completely off guard, the sight of Sylvia sitting in Edith's room was enough to unleash a whoosh of

147

adrenaline through Grace's body. She was cornered. Stay calm, she instructed herself silently as she opened the door wide enough to walk in. Forming her features into what she hoped was a smile Grace closed the door and walked over.

'Hello,' she said, taking in both women.

Edith gave her version of a smile, as did Sylvia. 'Grace, good morning!'

'Uh huh, you too,' Grace said. 'Um do you want me to wait outside until you're finished? I have plenty of time.'

'Oh no, I came here especially to see you today,' Sylvia replied.

'Right,' Grace murmured. 'Did you want to talk to me about something?'

'No, no I was just going to sit in while you read and discussed today's story.'

'Okay,' Grace said uneasily, trying to ignore the welling butterflies in her stomach. Feeling under intense scrutiny she retrieved the book and took her customary position on the recliner, trying to ignore Sylvia's presence as she went about her normal routine. Once she got as comfortable as was possible in the chair she looked over at Edith. 'Ready?' she asked.

She took Edith's blink as a yes.

Jake Harmon slid his Visa card through the reader on the ATM and waited with bated breath as it registered. Having trekked almost five kilometres on foot to the RSL specifically to use this slide-through machine, he prayed it would work. Both his debit cards had been swallowed by regular ATMs and he wasn't prepared to let this last link with a financial institution crumble as well.

The transaction screen appeared. So far, so good. How much should he get? Jake knew he was close to his limit, but this card had an overdraft facility. Was it worth the risk to get an extra two hundred? He decided it was. Keying in five hundred dollars, Jake hunched over the machine and waited. Beads of sweat popped up on his brow as the machine wheezed and hummed. It never usually took this long did it?

Jake's breathing started to quicken as he envisaged an alarm sounding and a hefty security guard appearing to escort him and his delinquent card away. Tapping his foot impatiently Jake glanced around the foyer. The door wasn't too far away. If there was a problem he could take off before anybody realised what was going on.

The tap on his shoulder caused him to jump violently. 'What?' he snapped at the skinny red-haired man who had appeared behind him.

'Hey, steady on buddy, you dropped your card.'

'Right,' Jake answered, holding out his hand to accept his Visa. 'Sorry, I'm just a bit jumpy.'

'I reckon everyone is these days. Ever since they installed those damned cameras. It's a sad day when you can't even pop down to the RSL without big brother tracking every move.'

The sweat was running down Jake's face now and his mouth as dry as the Sahara. 'Cameras?' he croaked.

'Yeah, security cameras. Don't you read your newsletter? The whole place is crawling with them.'

Ten more seconds and then I'm leaving, Jake decided

as he wiped his sweaty palms on his jeans. He had counted down to three when the cash slot finally opened and ten precious fifty dollar notes appeared. Jake snatched them up quickly, in case the machine should suddenly change its mind, shoved them in his shirt pocket and bolted directly for the exit.

• • • • •

Jake had always known what he did was wrong.

Of course at the time he had worked hard to push the thought away, reassuring himself that in such a buoyant economy pyramid schemes didn't *really* hurt anybody because there were always plenty of new investors ready to jump on board.

Deep down though the truth niggled at him, much like his tennis elbow that ebbed and flowed but never really went away. Plenty of booze filled nights out, extravagant shopping expeditions and luxurious holidays had certainly helped him deny his gut feelings. As did mixing with the sort of people who seemed to genuinely believe it was okay to operate outside the law, that the restrictions in the finance sector only rewarded mediocrity and stifled those with vision and the courage to try something new.

So when things came crashing down – when Jake was fired and his assets frozen, when his car and house were repossessed – he knew he didn't have a leg to stand on.

He was guilty and he was going down.

• • • • •

Later that night Jake sat on the cement floor of his former neighbour's garage, eating Homebrand Cornflakes straight from the box. Old Mrs Swinson didn't own a car and foolishly left the key under a pot plant outside the door. So far he had been able to sneak in and out without being noticed, but with each passing day the risk of discovery was increasing.

Shovelling another handful of cereal into his mouth, Jake pondered briefly the whereabouts of his former "investment partners". Although convicted of fraud, they had all managed to avoid actual jail time but had been banned from associating with each other ever again. Jake was happy enough to comply after being hung out to dry by the same people who had lured him into the whole mess in the first place.

Why did he always do that? Why did he let other people lead him into trouble? Why wasn't an honest job in corporate finance enough?

Emptying the last few cornflake crumbs into his mouth, Jake crushed the box and kicked it aside. The four hundred and eighty-five dollars currently in his possession was all he had left. It was another ten weeks before he was eligible for Centrelink benefits and his chances of obtaining employment were less than nil.

Leaning back against the fibro wall, Jake banged his head in frustration. He had spent the last two weeks desperately trying to formulate a plan to end the spiral his life was in. And unfortunately, amid all the possibilities, there was only one scenario that might work.

It wasn't something he wanted to do, who in their right

mind would? But desperate times called for desperate measures.

Wriggling into his sleeping bag Jake exhaled sharply. 'I can't believe it's come to this,' he muttered aloud, wishing the whole ordeal was over and his life could begin again.

• • • • •

When the weekend arrived Jake had finally psyched himself up for the task at hand. Working quietly in the dim light of the garage, he loaded several items into a small black backpack. He'd even made a list to make sure he didn't forget anything. Beanie, check. Cigarettes and lighter, check. Gun and bullets, check. Was this something only truly desperate people did? Jake wondered.

He had timed the journey at two hours and ten minutes and was aiming to arrive at 3.30 am when the service station and its surrounds would be quiet. Although he hadn't lived in the area for more than ten years, Jake had rung and confirmed it was still a twenty-four hour servo.

Glancing up at the house, he could see the lights on in the front and hear the TV blaring. A mad keen rugby league fan, Mrs Swinson would be immersed in the test match, which at least made leaving easier.

Zipping up his backpack, Jake eased out the door and closed it silently, before creeping down the driveway and out on to the street.

Arriving at his friend Glen's place at eleven thirty, Jake was relieved to see the car sitting in the driveway as arranged. With some time still to kill, he perched on the bonnet of the Falcon sedan. Twenty-five years old, it was technically un-roadworthy due to the rust patches that had begun to eat through the exterior and chassis, but was still registered.

An amateur mechanic and panel beater, Glen had got as far as replacing one of the doors and the top of the boot with panels sourced from the wreckers. Given that the original paintwork was an oxidised red and the replaced portions were white and canary yellow respectively, the effect was like a badly made patchwork quilt. However, the six cylinder engine was solid and according to Glen still had plenty of power, so Jake was prepared to overlook the aesthetics.

Glen had eyed Jake curiously when he had asked to borrow the car, but seemed to know better than to ask any questions beyond how long he wanted it for.

A black cat wandered into the yard and jumped on top of the wheelie bin, its bright green eyes watching Jake warily. He didn't know if its presence was of any significance as he ran through the sequence of events again in his mind. Jake knew he had made adequate preparations and like a student facing an exam, there was nothing more he could do but hope for the best.

The interior of the Falcon was in marginally better condition than the exterior, but only just. While the driver's seat was intact, the passenger side was a jumble of springs and foam and was jammed forward almost touching the dashboard. A selection of wires hung ominously beneath the steering wheel and the rear-view mirror was fastened to the roof via a piece of metal and a series of thick rubber bands. After poking it delicately with one finger and getting an impression of how fragile the structure was Jake decided to leave well enough alone.

Surprisingly the powerful engine started first go. Remembering Glen's warning about the tricky clutch, Jake eased it into gear and nosed on to the suburban street. Not wanting to draw attention to the un-roadworthy car, he was cautious with his speed as he made his way out of the suburbs but put his foot down once he made it to the highway.

Cruising along at a steady hundred, Jake selected a tape at random from the storage console between the two front seats and shoved it into the slot. Paul Kelly's *Dumb Things* blasted through the front speakers. Jake laughed at the appropriateness of the song title and started to sing along, 'In the middle, in the middle, in the middle of a dream. I lost my shirt, I pawned my rings I've done all the dumb things…'

Jake's off key singing was interrupted by a burst of static and the sounds of a tape being mangled.

'Bloody hell!' he exclaimed and hit the stop button. When that had no effect he pushed eject and the edge of the cassette appeared. Grasping it as best he could Jake pulled it out, relieved to see the trail of audio tape was still intact and could be wound back into the case. Throwing the tape onto the passenger seat, he flicked the stereo back to radio and spent thirty seconds moving through the pre-programmed stations, finally settling on the Saturday night request show on Cool Rock 105.3.

There wasn't much traffic on the road and each time another car appeared Jake wondered where they were going on this clear August night. He was fairly sure none of them were doing what he was.

Exhaling loudly he shook his head. Jake had always thought that criminals were evil people, who did bad things just for the hell of it. Now he realised that wasn't true. Sure, some of them might be evil, but most were probably just like him, victims of circumstance. One bad decision had led to a downward spiral that couldn't be reversed without a bold move on his part.

Although it had been a long time since he had been in the area, when Jake passed the abandoned sawmill he knew he was almost there. He had spent many hours of his childhood playing there, diving into piles of sawdust and building cubby houses with timber. It was now fenced off and there didn't appear to be much of the original structure left.

Although there were no cars on either side of the highway, Jake dutifully indicated as he turned into the driveway of McGill's Service Station. It had been upgraded and now had modern bowsers instead of the old fashioned ones he remembered. The shop had also been enlarged and fully renovated.

'Damn!' Jake exclaimed, as he pulled into one of the parking spots. There were people here. A red Daihatsu Charade was filling up at bowser four and a blue Torana was reversing over to the air pump.

Although he wanted it all over and done with, Jake found himself willing the other customers to take their time so he didn't have to make his move yet. He watched the overweight forty-something man with a drooping handlebar moustache climb out of the Torana. Picking up the tangled air hose, the man grappled with it for several seconds before unravelling it, then squatted down and attached it to his back left tyre.

The view at bowser four was much better. A young blonde woman wearing tight jeans and a white halter top was filling her tank and text messaging at the same time, obviously having never received the email about mobile phones and petrol pump explosions. Neither of them seemed to be in a hurry nor did they appear to notice Jake sitting in the dark. The young woman drove off first, gunning her engine and squealing her tyres as she sped out the driveway heading north. Mr Air Pump fiddled around for another five minutes, apparently getting each tyre to its perfect PSI before also heading north, albeit much more sedately.

Unzipping the backpack, Jake pulled the gun out and took a close look at it. Sure, it was nearly thirty years old but it was still in mint condition. In fact it had never been used. As a child he had longed to play with it, to shoot Coke cans off the fence like the other kids did, but couldn't bring himself to do it. Subconsciously he had always known it was cursed. But now he had to look beyond that.

Jake pulled his beanie low over his forehead and took several deep breaths before cracking the door. Once outside he stood there for another minute or two, scanning the outside road and straining his ears for any noise in the silent, clear night. The stars stood out in the sky like diamonds in a black velvet box and Jake made a wish upon one before walking over to the servo shop and opening the door.

The young attendant was engrossed in whatever he was watching on TV through the open office door and only glanced up briefly as Jake strode purposefully in ... and headed for the drinks fridge. Staring through the glass door at the bottles of Pepsi, Fanta, Sprite and Mount Franklin Water he shook his head in disgust at his own cowardice. So much for heading straight to the counter!

Glancing at the teenager at the register, Jake's stomach knotted. He couldn't expect people to understand that he HAD to do this; it wasn't just something he had decided on the spur of the moment. He had tried other ways to solve his problems but they hadn't worked. In truth when he'd finally made the decision to go through with it he had felt a sense of relief. But he hadn't expected to be this nervous.

The phone rang. Jake jumped violently in fright. The attendant answered on the second ring and launched into an animated conversation, apparently with his girlfriend going by the comments he was making.

'Yeah, yeah you do that. No, wear the red one.' He laughed heartily at something and then whispered into the receiver.

Jake willed the conversation to go on and on. He couldn't really be expected to hang around for an hour if they kept talking, could he?

But, of course, then attendant became a diligent worker and curtailed the conversation. 'All right, see you in the morning,' he said, before hanging up the phone.

Another customer came in then, a truck driver this time, decked out in King Gee workwear and a Brisbane Broncos beanie. Grabbing a cellophane wrapped pie out of the warmer and a bottle of chocolate milk from the fridge, he threw a suspicious glance at Jake before heading up to the counter.

Right Jake, you've got two minutes more and then you're doing it!

After studying the selection of road maps, then meandering around the chips display (and noting the two new Smiths flavours on offer), Jake pulled himself together. It was now or never and he hadn't come all this way for nothing. Pulling his beanie even lower over his face, Jake marched across the shop, looked the attendant right in the eye and dumped the contents of his bag on the counter.

Staring at Jake in shock, the attendant threw his hands into the air. 'Ooooh M-m-man,' he stammered, 'not again. Take it easy there mate.'

'I'm cool,' Jake replied. 'But I just need you to listen to me.'

'Oh, I'm listening, but to save us some time here I need to tell you the safe is on time lock. I honestly cannot open it. You can have what's in the till and the smokes, but seriously it's not that much.'

'I don't want anything – I want to give *you* something.'

'Let me guess, a bullet in the face just for the hell of it?'

'No, no, you've got it all wrong.'

When Jake made no move to pick the gun up, the attendant peered at it more closely, dropping his hands as he did so. 'All right, you had me there for a second, but we both know that's not a real gun.'

'No, it's not, it's a toy.'

Relaxing a little more, the attendant looked at the gun again. 'It's a beauty though, I've never seen one quite like that before.'

'Yeah it was top of the line in its day. All the kids wanted one.'

'I hate to break it to you buddy, but that's a pretty lame hold up attempt. You didn't even point the thing at me.' He motioned to the ceiling, 'You should know that we've got security cameras, and the cops don't take too kindly to people who bring guns into servos, even toy ones.'

Jake shook his head. 'I'm not trying to hold you up.'

'Okaaay, glad we've established that. So what's with all this?' the attendant asked, surveying the items on the counter. 'Liquorice bullets, two packets of Benson and Hedge's Extra Mild, a lighter and some cash. I take it there's a reason behind all this?'

Jake nodded. 'Twenty-eight years ago one of my friends and I came in to this service station one night. The guy who was on duty had to go outside and help someone and we stole this toy gun, a packet of liquorice bullets, two packets of cigarettes and a lighter. The guy didn't even see us leave and we never got caught.'

The attendant raised his eyebrows. 'Great story and really not that exciting. I've stolen way more than that and

159

never been caught either. Despite what those security posters say most shoplifters *do* get away with their crimes.'

'Ah, but *not being caught* and *getting away with it* are two different things. If you believe in karma, then you know that any wrong deed will return to you in some form.' Glancing at the young man's name badge Jake continued, 'You see Angus, I've completely trashed my life in the past two years and the only way I can get it back to rights is to confess to and make amends for every bad deed I've done. This was where my life of crime officially began.'

'Let me guess, your name is Earl?' Angus quipped.

'No, it's Jake, but I see you're familiar with the concept of karma?'

'Sure, kind of.'

'Then you know what I'm trying to do.'

'I guess so,' Angus replied. 'I'm assuming you want me to keep this stuff?'

'Yes, I do.'

'But I don't own the place, I just work here. It wasn't my stuff you stole.'

'I know,' Jake explained patiently. 'This is kind of symbolic. I tried to find the owner but I couldn't, so I just had to bring it back to the place.'

'What do I do with it?' Angus asked.

Jake shrugged. 'Put it on the shelves to sell?'

'We don't stock any of this stuff. You'd have to be nuts to sell a toy gun in a servo these days, we only sell Allen's confectionary and my boss hates Benson and Hedges. Apparently they screwed him over on some promotion twenty years ago. Something about a box of fake gold lighters that never arrived.'

'All right give it away, keep it for yourself, you choose.'

'What's with the cash? You didn't get any fuel.'

'The money is the cost of the things I stole at the time multiplied by the CPI and adding in a fair rate of interest if the money had been invested over the past twenty-five years.'

Angus counted the pile of notes and coins. 'Two hundred and forty-seven dollars and forty-five cents'

'It was actually forty-one cents, but I rounded up.'

'Awesome.'

'Hey just humour me here will you Angus? Obviously you think I'm nuts and that's your prerogative, but believe me the only way to cancel out negative energy is to create positive energy to go in its place. The universe doesn't forget.'

Angus raised his eyebrows. 'Whatever you reckon. Looks like I'm in for some tough times then.'

Jake shrugged. 'You don't have to be, it's all about choices.'

'Cool, I'll remember that.' Angus eyed Jake again and smirked. 'What's with the beanie?'

'I was wearing a beanie that night, just trying to recreate things accurately.'

'Right,' Angus said, still smirking. 'I reckon this cash is going to go right in my pocket.'

'That's okay. I've done my part giving it back; the karma ball is in your court now.'

Angus stood in a way that shielded him from the security camera, folded the notes and shoved them under the counter. 'That's a nice stash of drinking money.'

'Like I said, it's your choice,' Jake said, extending his hand. 'Thanks for letting me right a wrong.'

Angus shook Jake's hand exaggeratedly. 'No problem I guess, and good luck with all your other good deeds,' he said in a tone that Jake thought to be rather insincere.

As he walked out of the shop, Jake could feel the Angus' wryly amused gaze upon him, but he didn't care. He'd actually done it!

Feeling like a weight had been removed from his shoulders he smiled and nodded at the imposing bald cab driver who was filling up at bowser three. The cabbie ignored him but Jake shrugged it off.

Tomorrow was a whole new day.

• • • • •

Sylvia was smiling as Grace finished reading. 'Oh my goodness, what an interesting little story! I really didn't see that ending coming, did you?'

Edith shook her head slightly but Grace raised her eyebrows. 'Well to be honest, I sort of did.'

Sylvia's expression conveyed her surprise. 'Wow, you must be a very astute young lady. I guess I just followed the clues laid out and didn't consider any other possibility.'

'Yes, well I was like that at the start too, but then each week I've come to realise that each one of these stories has a twist somewhere. I didn't guess exactly what was going to happen but I was fairly sure he wasn't just going to rob the place.'

'So you've enjoyed the stories then?'

'Yes I have,' Grace admitted. 'I mean I wouldn't have minded whatever Edith wanted me to read, but it was a bonus to actually really invest in each story and try and work out where it was going to lead.'

'That's wonderful Grace! So you would say you've gained some wisdom along the way?'

'Yes,' Grace said. 'I suppose I have.'

'Well, that can only be a bonus, right?'

Grace nodded, surprised that her anxiety level had dropped quite substantially.

'Don't let me stop your normal post-mortem then. Go on as you normally would.'

Grace blanched a little at Sylvia's choice of words but did as she suggested. 'Well I really understood why Jake tried to make things right. I mean he did something really bad and he deserved to get punished, but I don't think the world works like that.'

Sylvia's gaze was intense. 'Oh?'

'No, I think once you do something really bad you kind of deserve to live with it forever. And if bad things happen because of it then you need to accept that.'

'Even if you just did something stupid on the spur of the moment and have regretted it ever since?' Sylvia asked.

Grace nodded sharply. 'Yes. Some things are unforgiveable.'

'Oh I don't know Grace, I like to think that karma is real enough. If you've done something wrong and are truly sorry for it and do something constructive to make up for it I really believe that the universe gives you another chance to get it right.'

Although Grace did her best to slip out of the room quietly, Sylvia apparently had other plans. 'Wait up Grace, I'll walk you out,' she said, moving the spare chair back against the wall and following her into the hall.

'I really enjoyed that,' Sylvia said as they threaded their way around the afternoon tea trolley that was parked rather haphazardly outside room 43.

'Thanks,' Grace murmured. 'But I'm just the reader, the stories aren't mine.'

'Well, yes that's true enough,' Sylvia said, 'but it's not just about reading a story. The whole analysis thing you do is great and the way you involve Edith is really lovely too.'

'Really? Sometimes I feel like I'm being a bit insensitive when I complain or talk about things she can no longer do.'

Sylvia shook her head. 'No, don't think like that. There's literally nothing you can say to someone in Edith's position that isn't offensive in some way if you analyse it enough. Edith has been in here long enough to have developed an acceptance of her situation and she is past being overly sensitive to everyday conversation.'

'How does she do it?' Grace murmured, more to herself than to Sylvia.

Sylvia sighed softly. 'I wonder that myself sometimes. Working in aged care you have to develop a bit of thick skin to stop yourself getting burnt out, but Edith is one of those cases that just makes you shake your head in awe.'

'Yeah,' Grace agreed.

They had reached Sylvia's office. 'It was really nice to see you today Grace,' she said. 'To be honest I wasn't sure how you would go with Edith, but you're doing an amazing job.'

'Thanks.'

'I mean it Grace,' Sylvia said as she opened the door to her office. 'You should be very proud of yourself. See you next week.'

'Yeah, see you,' Grace echoed, unable to keep a smile from forming as she headed out to the exit.

* * * * *

The staff at the hospital had been surprised at how adamant Grace was about not contacting her family. They had wheedled and cajoled to the best of their abilities but none of them – the nurses, the social worker or even the head psychiatrist – could convince her to reveal her next of kin. Being over eighteen by the time she was admitted and therefore legally an adult, they had to accept her decision.

It wasn't that she didn't want to see them, to feel the warmth of their loving embrace and to pour out her woes like she once would have. The problem was she simply didn't deserve to. They had given up so much to support her dream and she had thrown in back in their faces.

Grace tried not to dwell too much on how the whole incident would have impacted on them. Small towns could be amazingly supportive but also heartbreakingly cruel when one of their own betrayed them so spectacularly. She could only hope the scar would heal with time and their lives could go on as they always had.

Still buoyed by Sylvia's praise the previous week, Grace was initially feeling positive as she signed the visitors register the following week. It was hard to believe it was her seventh visit and that she was past the midway point of her twelve week placement. The three months that had seemed like a lifetime when she was assigned to Rosehill Gardens now felt like it was slipping away much too quickly. Mild panic blossomed as she contemplated this fact, quickly suffocating the positivity she had been basking in just minutes before. The future suddenly loomed, scary and uncertain. What was to become of her after Rejoin finished? What was the next hurdle she would have to jump?

Frozen with inertia Grace might have stayed there all morning if the woman waiting behind her hadn't tapped her on the shoulder. 'Are you finished?' she asked briskly. 'I've got lots to get done today.'

'Sorry, yes go ahead,' Grace said, handing her the pen and stepping aside. Calm down, she instructed herself sternly. Worry about the future when it's a bit closer. You've got another six visits before you have to stress about all that.

Grace was happy to find Edith alone when she entered her room. As much as she liked Marion and had even coped fine with Sylvia being there the previous week, she really did prefer it when it was just the two of them. She spoke much more freely knowing Edith couldn't speak back. There was no chance of judgement wrapped up as encouragement or being offered trite words of advice.

'Hi Edith,' she said, giving the best smile she could manage.

Edith smiled back and gave a small nod.

'I love your hair.'

Another smile.

Grace still hadn't worked out if Edith's hair was real and if it was who styled it. Today it was wrapped into an elegant French twist and did indeed look lovely.

After settling herself into the least dippy bit of the chair, Grace picked up the book and realised they were getting close to the end. She wondered where they would get another book to read and made a mental note to ask Sylvia about it on her way out today.

Flipping the pages over, Grace finally reached the next title page, surprised to see that it simply read "Your Story". Furrowing her brow she turned the page over slowly, then the butterflies in her stomach started dancing ever faster as she noticed the following pages were blank. Realising what was happening she slowly raised her eyes and shook her head at Edith.

'I can't,' she whispered.

Edith held her gaze and nodded her head slowly and deliberately.

Grace shook her head again. 'You really don't want to hear it.'

Edith's gaze didn't waver and Grace realised she was not going to win this little standoff. Leaning back in the chair she closed her eyes for a moment before exhaling loudly. 'All right,' she agreed finally. 'I'll tell you, but only because you can't repeat it to anybody else.'

Edith nodded.

'Believe it or not I'm a pianist,' Grace began. 'I actually can't remember *not* being able to play the piano. I know that probably sounds a bit strange, because you've got to learn first, right? Not to mention practice a lot.'

Edith blinked.

'Well apparently most people do, but somehow I was born already knowing. We had this old shed on our farm that was a bit of a junk depository and one day when I was five I went in there and discovered an old piano that had belonged to my great grandparents. It was covered in dirt and cobwebs and was horrifically out of tune but I was immediately fascinated by it and started pinging away. I must have been in there for hours because Mum came looking for me. She was frantic; apparently she and Dad and my big brother had been calling out to me and searching everywhere. They were just about to organise a full-scale search when they heard the music.

'Mum was just about to tear strips off me when she realised I was playing a simplified version of one of the pieces from the classical CD she played all the time when she cooked. I can still remember the look on her face when she just stared at me wondering how on earth I could know how to do that.'

Edith shifted her head slightly and raised an eyebrow.

Grace shrugged. 'I know, it's weird hey? But as soon as I touched the keys something just guided my fingers. The music seemed to flow right from my brain to my hands. At that age I didn't realise it was something that not everybody could do. After that my parents immediately enrolled me in music lessons. My teacher, Mrs Pembroke, was determined that I would learn to read music, which came as a rude shock to start with. She took something that was natural and intrinsic to me and made it stiff and formal so I hated the lessons at first and still played by ear, just pretending to follow the notes on the page. But gradually I realised the value of being able to read music and started applying myself. Once I put some effort in I realised that it wasn't so hard after all.

'As good as everybody insisted I was at playing the piano, I hadn't really considered it as a career choice, beyond being a teacher myself. I certainly hadn't dreamed of being a performer, it had never even crossed my mind that I could do that.'

The door opened then and Max the afternoon tea person appeared. 'Good afternoon Edith,' the fifty something man boomed cheerfully, 'and Miss Grace too. How are you love?' he asked as he wheeled the trolley in.

'Fine thanks,' Grace replied, amazed that he remembered her name when she had met him only once before.

'Right, hot Milo for Edith,' he announced, and poured a prepared chocolate mix into a plastic beaker with a built in straw and placed it on the movable table next to Edith's bed, in a place she could lean over and drink from it. 'And I believe it's a coffee for you young Grace? I never forget a drink order,' he boasted.

Grace nodded. She didn't really like coffee; especially not the jar of instant she could see on the trolley but it was easier than saying she didn't want anything. Max dumped two teaspoons of Maxwell House in a melamine mug then splashed in some water and a drop of milk. 'There you go Grace,' he said. 'That'll get you through the rest of the day.'

Accepting the drink, Grace took a sip of the lukewarm liquid, careful not to recoil at the bitter, plastic taste.

'Thanks,' she said.

'So how is the story telling going today?' he asked conversationally, leaning on the trolley and smiling at the two of them.

'Great thanks,' Grace replied uneasily, panic rising at the idea he might stop and listen for a while.

'I love a good yarn myself,' he said, 'but duty calls. Enjoy your day.' He swung the trolley around and headed out the door.

Grace set her coffee down on the floor and glanced over at Edith. 'You aren't bored yet?'

Edith shook her head.

'Okay, where was I? Oh yeah I was talking about performing. It was Miss Bennett who opened my eyes as to what I might be able to do someday. She was a new graduate teacher who arrived when I was in Year Eleven and took me on as a bit of a special project. She said she didn't have the talent to make it to the top but reckoned she could spot it in somebody who did. And that was when Strauss Academy first appeared on my horizon.'

* * * * *

Strauss Academy did not offer scholarships. Founded by the wealthy Van der Linden family for the benefit of other wealthy families it had such an extensive waiting list that they simply didn't bother. But upon hearing they were urgently scouting for a lead pianist Miss Bennet had come up with a plan to circumvent the scholarship issue – a massive fund raising drive to come up with the tuition money for Grace's final year of school.

First they had to get through the interview. Miss Bennet had been amazing, drilling not only Grace but also her parents in how they should look and speak and more importantly what they should say to the snooty principal Ms Saskia Van der Linden. Having worked there as a dorm supervisor while she was at university Miss Bennet knew the ins and outs of the place and without her help Grace knew she never would have stood a chance.

Grace had been humbled at how her local community rallied to help her achieve her dream especially when so many of them had so little themselves. But that was what small towns did. They had done the same to send Gerry Mills on the professional rodeo circuit in America and had worked tirelessly to fund surgery to save Alice Wordley's sight. It was such a lot of money for just one year of schooling, but the doors it would open, well, that was where the value came in. Grace promised them faithfully she would work hard and do her little town proud and, would someday find a way to repay their kindness.

It had taken a while to adjust to her new school environment. Despite having the best of everything at her disposal and being surrounded by others just as passionate about music as she was, Grace found herself on a steep learning curve. While she enjoyed being in Brisbane and having the freedom to zip around town in her beloved new Peugeot, she still missed home and her family, desperately at times. And while she made new friends and enjoyed socialising with them it was a challenge to keep up the façade that had got her through the interview.

Raised to be scrupulously honest, Grace didn't like

playing fast and loose with the truth. Careful to never straight out lie, she let her fellow students believe she was the daughter of a wealthy grazier, rather than a struggling small crops farmer who counted himself lucky if he broke even after every harvest. At first she had lived in fear of slipping up, but soon realised that Huntley Valley was too far away to even have any relevance for her classmates.

As the first term moved on and her musical ability started to speak for itself Grace began to relax more. True to her promise to her community she worked hard, putting in long hours with her other academic subjects as well as her piano. Perhaps her greatest discovery was that she loved to perform. Unlike the nerve wracking experiences of the local and regional eisteddfods back home, being part of an accomplished orchestra was amazing and she felt for certain that her future would involve being on a stage somewhere, maybe even at an international level.

* * * * *

'It did take me a while to settle in,' Grace admitted, 'but eventually I did. I had never fully immersed myself in music before and Strauss allowed me to do that. There was an amazing freedom in being able to go to one of the practice rooms at six o'clock in the morning and bang out some scales or fine tune a performance piece without worrying about waking up the rest of the house. And the teachers there *expected* that music was your first priority and maths was just going through the motions.

'By the time the mid-year break came around I had really found my feet. I loved going home for the holidays to catch up with everybody but I was equally looking forward to going back to school. The way the year was structured we would finish our requirements for our non-music subjects in August and the rest of the year was dedicated to performance. We had our own season at the Performing Arts Centre as well as guesting for a month at the Sydney Opera House.'

Edith raised her eyebrows and gazed at Grace in surprise.

'I know; it was pretty amazing. I guess it was the privilege of paying fifty grand for a year of schooling. A lot of the other kids just took it for granted, but I really appreciated just how lucky I was. A few days before I went back to school the local paper did a story about me I guess to reassure everyone that the money they raised was being well spent. I didn't realise that larger newspapers could pick up stories from tiny newspapers out in the sticks so I had no qualms being completely open with the *Huntley Valley Chronicle* with its limited readership of 1200 because everyone knew me anyway. It wasn't until my Auntie Ruth in Brisbane rang in a state of great excitement that the first jolt of panic hit. *The Courier Mail* had picked up the story in its entirety. And I realised that I had been exposed.'

Once again Grace was interrupted by the sound of Max and his trolley making its way back down the hall. Hearing his voice through the thin walls of the room next door, Grace leant down to retrieve her coffee and dispose of it before he reappeared to collect the cups. Catching Edith's wryly amused glance, she smiled guiltily in return before reaching over the right armrest to dump the contents in the pot plant that sat in the corner of the room.

She wasn't sure what made her take a second glance at the unremarkable Formica topped table that housed the miniature fern, but it certainly felt that fate directed her gaze right to the concealed digital recording device strategically placed to best catch her voice. She didn't know which was worse – the icy spikes of shock or the hot rage of anger and betrayal that coursed through her veins simultaneously. All she knew was that she had to leave, immediately, before she said or did something she would regret.

Taking a second to glare at Edith, she forgot for a moment she was looking at a stroke victim in a nursing home and saw only a person who had betrayed her. Edith's expression was puzzled at first then paled as comprehension dawned. Grace was glad she was unable to speak as it meant she didn't have to listen to any excuses as she stomped over to the door. Ripping it open she didn't even look at Max as she slipped past the tea trolley and ran down the hallway.

The call came on a Wednesday – the day after the third visit to Edith that Grace had missed.

Enraged after discovering the recorder, as soon as she arrived home that day Grace had fired off an angry email to Sylvia, but had only received an out of office reply in response informing her Sylvia was on annual leave for a month. In typical Grace style she had dealt with the problem since by simply avoiding it but no doubt at some point she would be obliged to tell her case worker that she wasn't volunteering at Rosehill any more. So be it! They could assign her somewhere else, surely there were plenty of other nursing homes she could go to. No doubt there would be some fallout for not finishing Rejoin in the allotted time span, but there would be a way around it. She could always play the anxiety card to the max. People were so afraid of being sued these days they would never dare push a person in a fragile mental state too hard.

Grace felt a little frisson of shame at that thought. It sounded just a tad manipulative; all right it was very manipulative. But you had to do what you needed to stay in the system and get the support you needed and she certainly wouldn't be the first to do it.

That doesn't make it okay though, the good Grace argued.

Tired of trying to referee these thoughts, Grace reached for the TV remote to dull them down and picked up her phone by mistake. It then proceeded to ring in her hand, startling her. Giving herself a moment to calm down, Grace answered on the eighth ring.

'Hello.' Her voice was barely a whisper.

'Grace?' the voice on the other end asked tentatively.

'Yes.'

'It's Ellen Murphy here, I'm the Centre Manager at Rosehill Gardens.'

'Oh.' The Centre Manager! She must really be in trouble.

'I'm just calling about Edith,' Ellen continued.

Although she had plenty of excuses at the ready, including a defensive attack about Edith's (and Sylvia's) deception, Grace could not immediately articulate what was on her mind. 'I, uh, I … found the recorder,' she began. 'They tricked me you see, I didn't know—'

Ellen cut her off before she could say anything else. 'Grace, that's not important.'

'Does she want to see me again?' Grace asked, becoming more annoyed and articulate as she went on. Fancy calling in the Centre Manager. That was a bit of a mean trick. Edith was clearly very well regarded by the staff but Grace never imagined she would use it to her advantage like this. 'I can't come back,' she blustered. 'I know she's very ill and I should cut her some slack but—'

'Grace,' Ellen cut in, 'Please just listen to me. I'm not calling because of any problem or disagreement; I'm calling because Sylvia said you would want to know.'

So riled up and consumed with her own thoughts, Grace she missed the end of Ellen's sentence. 'Sorry, what did you say?'

Ellen's voice was firm but gentle. 'Edith is gone Grace.'

It was like one of those sucker punches people talked about. It came right out of nowhere and struck Grace smack in the middle of her solar plexus. 'What?' she gasped.

'She's gone Grace,' Ellen repeated. 'We lost her

yesterday.'

'I don't understand! She was okay last time I saw her.'

'Yes, well, she had another setback and there was nothing we could do. We did fear it might happen.'

'But we parted on bad terms, I didn't get to say goodbye,' Grace cried.

'That's the way it goes sometimes, unfortunately,' Ellen said kindly. 'I've spoken at length with Sylvia and she spoke very highly of you and the wonderful rapport you and Edith shared. She genuinely loved having you visit her. Just focus on those good memories and know that you helped her enjoy her last few weeks with us.'

An overwhelming sense of loss hit Grace then and she started to cry – noisy, gut-wrenching sobs that caused her thin body to shudder violently. 'S-s-s-o-orry,' she hiccupped.

'Don't be,' Ellen replied patiently. 'Take all the time you need. I'll be here when you've calmed down a bit.'

Eventually Grace regained her composure enough to talk to Ellen again. 'Thank you for telling me.'

'That's all right Grace. It's been a shock for all of us but as I said Sylvia was most insistent that you should know.'

'Tell her thank you.'

'I will Grace, I will. But you are going to need to speak to her yourself eventually.'

It felt strange to meet in a café rather than at Rosehill. Standing on the threshold of The Coffee Club in the city Grace peered inside, looking for Sylvia. Dressed casually in skinny jeans and a hoodie and with her hair in a ponytail, it took Grace a moment to recognise the other woman. Looking up from her iPhone she waved Grace over.

'Hi Grace, it's really nice to see you,' she said with a smile.

'Hello,' Grace murmured eyes downcast. The sting of betrayal still needled and she wasn't prepared to brush everything under the carpet just because Edith was gone.

'Did you order something?' Sylvia asked.

Grace shook her head.

'I can get you something if you like?'

Grace shook her head again. 'No I'm fine. I've got my water,' she replied, pulling a battered Mount Franklin bottle out of her bag and setting it on the table.

Sylvia sighed. 'All right Grace, I'm sorry it's taken this long to get back to you about the email you sent. As you can understand the loss of Edith obviously had to take precedence over everything else that was happening. And of course I was on leave when you sent it so I've only just recently had the opportunity to catch up on all that kind of stuff.'

'Uh, huh.'

'Grace I just want you to know I have a lot of sympathy for you and what you've been through. I know you feel your privacy has been violated by me knowing so many of your personal details but it was necessary so that we could make the most of your placement at Rosehill. I'm not one of those administrators who takes programs like Rejoin

181

lightly. If I put my name to it I do it properly.'

'And that includes spying on people without their knowledge? Tricking them into revealing things to a person who can't speak who they think is safe to talk freely to?'

The waitress with Sylvia's chai latte interrupted them briefly. 'Thanks,' Sylvia said with a smile.

'No worries,' the teenager replied cheerily. 'Let me know if you need anything else. You can refill your bottle over at the fountain if you like,' she said to Grace, motioning to the far wall.

'Okay,' Grace replied.

Sylvia stirred her drink slowly before scooping some froth off the top. 'I can understand you feeling the way you do,' she said, pausing to lick her spoon, 'but you've really got the wrong end of the stick.'

'I'm not sure how there can be a right end to this particular stick,' Grace countered, taking a sip of water.

'I'm not happy that this has distressed you Grace, but I can't help being pleased that it has brought you out of yourself. You barely looked at me that first day we met and now you look like you could happily rip my head off.'

'It's just really hard when you feel like other people are making all the decisions about your life.'

'We'll get to Rejoin in a minute, for now I just want to explain about the whole recording thing.'

'I'm all ears.'

'As I told you on your first visit, Edith used to be an English teacher and she loved to read and write. She had lots of different volunteers read to her while she was with us. It was a deliberate thing on her part as she liked to engage with a wide range of people.'

'Okay.'

'Anyway back when she could still talk she mentioned to me one day how so many of her volunteers just liked to chat after reading and that many of them had really interesting stories to tell. We came up with a plan to record each person's story, then Edith would work on it with an old teaching colleague of hers to create a short story. It was a great project as it kept her brain busy and let her do something she loved to do.'

'So all the stories I read were true?'

Sylvia took another sip of latte. 'Yeah, more or less. Edith and her friend changed the names and enough details to protect the identity of each person but they are based on real experiences.'

'But they've all got that twist you don't see coming.'

'That's right. Edith was a big believer that if you looked at any event the right way there was an unexpected element in it somewhere. That was the challenge for her, to work it in such a way that it fit the same format.'

Grace's eyes widened. 'So you've met all those people?'

'Yes I have. Well versions of them. That's the amazing thing about the volunteer roster at a nursing home, you really do get all types.'

Grace started fiddling with the lid on her water bottle, twisting it back and forth. 'So she did that without telling them?'

'Oh no, no, not at all. Of course we asked them.'

'But you didn't ask me.'

Sylvia averted her gaze for a moment then looked Grace in the eye. 'You're right Grace, we should have asked first. But you were a bit of a special case. Edith had this idea that she could re-write the ending of your story to inspire you to start really living your life again. But she needed to hear the background first.'

A thought struck Grace and she looked at Sylvia sharply. 'How could she do that if she couldn't speak or type?'

'Her friend had an iPad with some pretty amazing apps. They worked out a system.'

'It's a shame I didn't finish telling it,' Grace murmured. 'But then again I doubt even Edith could have fashioned a happy ending. Only a fairy godmother with magical powers could create a twist that would somehow make my life turn out okay.'

Sylvia pushed her empty cup away and sat up straighter, looking more businesslike as she did so. 'That's where you're wrong Grace. I have a lot of sympathy for the bad times you have endured, but you're only twenty years old. You cannot let yourself get sucked into the system and spend the rest of your life defending your right to live a life that nowhere near meets your potential.'

Grace was already shaking her head. 'I can't lose my disability payment!'

Sylvia's tone was kind but firm. 'Yes you can. Even though you didn't finish Rejoin I've seen enough to make my recommendation. I'm not ticking the box that says "continued disability support required", I'm categorising you as work ready.'

'I can't,' Grace repeated with tears running down her cheeks. 'It's too humiliating to apply for job after job and be asked each time why I didn't finish school. It just makes me more depressed! I don't have enough confidence to go to work; didn't you read the report from the Mental Health Alliance? It says I will never be able to function normally. How can I—'

'Grace,' Sylvia interrupted, 'That report was filed to get you maximum assistance when you were in a crisis situation. It does not have to define your life going forward. Besides, the rules have changed in an effort to stop young people like you ending up reliant on welfare.'

'My case worker won't agree with it.'

'I've spoken at length with your case worker and she's with me on this. It's time for you to make your way into the world Grace, you've got too much to offer to stay a hermit forever.'

'You're being so unfair,' Grace sobbed. 'Who will ever employ me?'

Sylvia reached over and gently lifted Grace's chin so she was looking at her. 'I will Grace. I want you to come and work for me at Rosehill. But first you have to tell me what happened at Strauss.'

Shocked not only at the job offer but also at what she was asking, Grace stared at Sylvia. 'But you already know don't you?'

'No I don't. All your paperwork tells me is your diagnosis; it doesn't tell me what caused the nervous breakdown.'

'Really? I thought they told you everything. That's why I could never look at you.'

Sylvia shook her head.

Grace sat up straighter and folded her arms before levelling her gaze at Sylvia. 'Well I assume you know the first part that I told Edith.'

Sylvia's face reddened. 'Uh, yes I did listen to the recording,' she admitted.

Grace raised her eyebrows and let the words hang in the air a moment before answering. 'All right, fine, I'll tell you. But I'll need a proper drink first.'

Sylvia couldn't hide her shock. 'But it's only 9.30 am!'

'No, I mean something decadent like a white hot chocolate with cream and extra marshmallows.'

Sylvia was already on her feet. 'Coming right up.'

It was a subdued and very nervous Grace who returned to school after the mid-year break. Having gotten hold of a copy of *The Courier Mail* in question she was relieved to find her story was buried in the Arts section and was not the front page headline her Auntie Ruth's reaction had suggested. Still it was out there now, her authentic self in all its glory. It wasn't the paper's fault of course; they thought they were doing something nice by celebrating a small town girl who had been given an amazing leg up in her chosen field.

Rather than arriving back on Saturday afternoon as planned, Grace left her return to the last possible moment, slinking in at nine o'clock on Sunday night and heading straight to her room before anybody saw her. At least having her own room meant she could hide away as long as necessary. Sure, she would have to attend classes and practice but at least she could avoid the common room.

Climbing into bed she buried her head under the pillow to bock out the excited chatter of classmates in their surrounding rooms and steeled herself to ride out the semester ahead alone and friendless if she needed to. All that mattered was getting through the year and making Huntley Valley proud.

It took Grace a couple of days to realise that she had worried for nothing. Her friends greeted her with open arms, eager to hear about her holidays. No mention was made of the article, and no insults or taunts were slung her way. The reason why didn't strike her until she was standing at the breakfast buffet several days later. After scooping some fruit salad into her bowl, she didn't shake the ladle completely and trailed sticky juice along the crisp white tablecloth and on to the stack of newspapers that was delivered each morning; the stack of newspapers the students walked past at every meal but never picked up.

Teenagers don't read newspapers! she realised with a jolt. If they even bothered with the news at all they read it on their iPad or phone. And only the main news items made it onto the website, not the supplements. In addition, a fair portion of Strauss' students came from interstate, and a few from overseas. Nobody had even seen the piece!

Grace resisted the urge to break into a happy dance as an overwhelming sense of relief swept over her. It was like the day she passed her driving test or when she received a distinction for AMusA. She knew she shouldn't feel so relieved that her true background remained hidden, but she was a pragmatist if nothing else. Sometimes you had to work the system to get what you wanted and needed and if playing a little fast and loose with the truth wasn't hurting anybody then she could certainly live with it.

* * * * *

Sylvia had worked her way through her second chai latte by now and watched Grace as she paused to nibble on a marshmallow. The barista had gone all out when Sylvia asked for extras, presenting five marshmallows on a saucer with a fancy doily in addition to the two in her drink.

'I went to the library and looked up the digital file of your newspaper story,' Sylvia admitted. 'It was a really nice piece.'

'Yeah it was. I'm not proud of the fact I wanted to hide

it from my friends at Strauss, but you know important it is to fit in at school. I just wanted to graduate and then I didn't care what anyone thought.'

'I understand totally Grace, I'm not judging you.'

'In hindsight, I don't think the other kids would really have cared that much. Sure, they were all rich kids and it was a very exclusive environment, but the reality was we were all music nerds. At any other normal school we would have been the outcasts, the weird kids who spent all their spare time practising instead of partying.'

Sylvia nodded thoughtfully. 'That's a good point.'

Grace picked up another marshmallow. 'But that doesn't explain why I went off the deep end though, does it?'

'A breakdown isn't going off the deep end.'

'Oh yes it is. Well that's what it feels like anyway. It's like jumping off the highest diving platform and realising you have no safety net and nobody to catch you at the bottom.'

'I'm sorry you had to go through that Grace, but yes I am still wondering why?'

'Fair enough. Here comes the ugly part.'

* * * * *

The semester was five weeks old before Ms Van der Linden arrived back on campus. Fresh from a month long sabbatical at their sister school in Vienna she exuded warmth and enthusiasm as she addressed the student body at Monday assembly. Grace felt her attention wander as she listened to the stick thin, peroxide blonde espouse her own special brand of wisdom. Yes of how her time in Vienna had confirmed what she already knew – that the finest musical achievement was born only in exclusive institutions such as theirs. Bla, bla, bla…

Grace had disliked Ms Van der Linden from the moment she had realised that she needed to play a role in order to attend Strauss, that she wasn't there on her musical talent alone. Four months to go Grace, she reminded herself as the principal continued to speak. For all her grand speeches about music and her penchant for dropping in on practice sessions, Grace had never perceived any true musical passion from the older woman. In fact, she had begun to suspect that Ms Van der Linden did not even play a musical instrument. No musician she knew had perfectly manicured fingernails or could stand impassive in a performance room without showing some kind of emotion at the beauty of orchestral music.

The sound of the school song brought Grace back to the present. Standing with her fellow students she sang proudly, glad to be where she was despite having so little respect for the woman up on the podium.

It was when Grace was in hospital that the psychiatrist had used the analogy of the frog. Dr Wayne Baker was not known for his dress sense. Stuck in the eighties, at around fifty he still wore stonewash denim and skinny ties. But he was a kind man and Grace knew he was trying his very best to help her.

'If you drop a frog in boiling water it'll hop right back out quick smart,' Dr Baker explained during one of his visits. 'But if you put it in a pan of cold water and gradually heat it up the frog will stay in there, not realising it is gradually being heated until it's too late. That's how a mental health crisis can occur. You just accept all the little things and then one day you realise you are in a pot of boiling water with no way out.'

Grace hadn't full appreciated the wisdom of that story until later. Looking back she could see that was exactly what had happened to her and just how cleverly it had been executed.

The early incidents were small enough as to be seen as insignificant. Being unfairly blamed for leaving the studio door unlocked, her car door getting keyed, a major assignment she had handed in going missing and having the unsettling feeling that someone had been in her room during the day were not pleasant but were easy enough to shrug off. But then things started to escalate.

First her personal coach was changed. So far into the year there was no logic in such a change and neither she or the coach were told why, beyond that the management committee stated that the new pairing was a better fit. They were not, in fact far from it, but to avoid making waves Grace had gritted her teeth and gotten on with it, considering herself experienced enough to polish her own performances.

Next, her practice blocks were changed to all evening. While this could sometimes happen in the junior school and was considered a rite of passage it was unheard of for seniors. When she questioned the change she was called into the principal's office and told to toughen up. 'Get used to it,' Ms Van der Linden had sneered, 'the performance world is not for the weak willed.' Hating how isolated this new schedule made her feel but seeing no alternative, Grace once again put her head down and toughed it out.

Slowly the combination of the two factors began to take its toll. Her new coach Mrs Morley was a tyrant, who stood over Grace's left shoulder at every practice session and slowly pecked away at her self-confidence. The evening practice sessions ran longer, leaving her exhausted and with little time to complete her other homework. This in turn necessitated her getting up early in the morning to catch up despite being so tired.

* * * * *

Intrigued by what she was hearing, Sylvia said, 'I'm going to read between the lines and guess it was Ms Van der Linden who was behind all this?'

Grace nodded slowly. 'Uh huh. Her secretary Mrs Adams had seen the article and kept it for her, thinking it was a nice story about the school. But Ms VDL didn't see it that way. Her spin on it was that she had been deceived and that Strauss' reputation was sullied as a result.'

'Seriously?'

'Yep. Not that she ever confronted me about it. Instead she just kept tormenting me in her own special way.'

'So how did you find out?'

'Mrs Adams told me one day when I ended up in sick bay because I was so exhausted. She apologised, saying that she never would have given the article to her if she'd known how she would react.'

'So it all came to a head eventually?'

Grace nodded slowly.

'Sorry to bring it all up again.'

'That's okay. It's time somebody knew the whole story.'

* * * * *

With hindsight it was a stupid thing to do, but to a seventeen year old who was burning the candle at both ends and suffering massive stress, pep pills seemed like a great short-term solution. With academic exams just a week away and the constant pressure of practice, Grace was desperate for something to get her over this hump. Once she could do away with her other subjects she knew she would be able to make it to the September holidays. After two weeks at home to restore her equilibrium she knew she would be able to embrace the performance block that awaited them all.

The crazy thing was she only took them once. One episode of being wide awake for twenty-four hours and listening to the sound of her racing heart throughout her maths exam was more than enough for Grace. Tossing them aside, she soldiered on the old fashioned way and made it through exam week under her own steam.

Walking out of her history exam should have been a moment of jubilation for Grace, knowing that all her academic subjects were over and done with. Instead it was the most shameful experience of her life, being met by the principal who was holding the box of pills the cleaner had found in her room.

* * * * *

'All right it was a silly thing to do,' agreed Sylvia, 'but it wasn't like you were busted with cocaine or something.'

'Yeah, well the way Ms Van der Linden was looking at me you would have thought I was cooking up crystal meth in my room.'

'So what did she say?'

'At that point nothing. She just told me to be in her office in an hour.'

'Alright what did she say *then*?'

'Well, I was certain she was going to tell me I was expelled, and I couldn't face that. So I just took off.'

'What? You just left everything behind and drove away?'

'Pretty much.'

'I'm assuming you didn't go home then?'

'No, definitely not. I stayed in Brisbane.'

'But surely your parents could have helped?'

'Looking back now yes I'm sure they could have. But in that moment I was so ashamed of failing everybody that I wasn't thinking straight. Leaving seemed to be the only option.'

Sylvia shook her head. 'Oh Grace.'

'I found a cheap place to stay. It was horrible and the landlord was really creepy but as long as I paid my rent he left me alone. I felt terrible using the rest of my spending money that way and I had to sell my car but I didn't have a lot of choice. At first I thought I could find a way to sort everything out. I even rang Mrs Adams a few times and she begged me to come in. I almost caved when she told me how worried my parents were but then she let it slip how furious everyone was that I mucked up all the performance arrangements. Then I knew I couldn't go back.'

'Grace you do realise you probably wouldn't have been expelled over that? Sure pep pills are bad news but they're not illegal. Besides, you were an integral part of the orchestra.'

'Yeah I do know that now but back then I was certain she would kick me out. I was already so physically and emotionally exhausted I wasn't in the right frame of mind to make any kind of decisions, let alone big ones like that.'

'And of course one bad choice leads to another…'

'Yep. And the longer it goes on the harder it is to see any kind of way out of the situation.'

'I'm guessing things spiralled out of control after that?'

'Yeah you could say that. I was kind of holding my own at first; I even got a job at Coles to help me stay afloat. But then the panic attacks started. They were so incredibly scary and I just didn't know how to deal with them. I had a really severe one at work one day and collapsed. They called an ambulance and I ended up in hospital for five months.'

'Didn't the hospital contact your family?'

'I wouldn't let them. I just refused to give any contact details.'

'And you haven't thought of getting in touch since?'

'I've written them a few letters to let them know I'm okay, but it's been too long now. I'm just hoping everyone in town has forgiven them for being associated someone who wasted all their hard earned money.'

Sylvia was shaking her head now. 'Grace! You can't believe that. Honestly?'

'Yeah I do. My part of the bargain was graduating from Strauss and then going on to university or the conservatorium. I folded under the pressure and I blew it. The people who supported me have every right to be ropable about that.'

Sylvia picked up her phone and touched the Safari icon then googled white pages. Clicking on the link she navigated to the search field and then started typing. 'Okay surname McDonald, town Huntley Valley.'

Grace's eyes widened. 'What are you doing?'

'Is your parents' address 85 Hennessy Road?'

Even though Grace vehemently shook her head, Sylvia could tell by her reaction that the answer was yes. Double tapping the number to copy it she closed Safari and created a new contact. Holding the phone so Grace could see the call screen with the number entered she looked the young woman in the eyes firmly but kindly.

'All right Grace this ends right now. Either you call them or I will.'

Two Years Later

Grace

Grace sat at the piano trying her hardest to control her breathing. Her ragged gasps felt like she was in the middle of a severe asthma attack. But that was ridiculous, she wasn't asthmatic, not even mildly so. Her whole family had been tested when her brother was diagnosed and the doctor had assured her she possessed a perfectly healthy set of lungs.

Trying to take her mind off what lay ahead Grace lifted the lid on the ageing upright Yamaha. Inhaling the distinctive scent of the instrument she loved, she skimmed her fingers across the ebony and ivory, willing them to calm her down. If only she could perform her presentation musically this afternoon. That she could do. Even with a captive audience in the stands and a spotlight upon her, performing was her happy place. Pachelbel's Canon in D or a bit of Handel or Bach would be just perfect as an accompaniment she decided before coming back to reality.

Reaching up to the pile of notes she had placed on top of the piano she looked over them one more time. Checking her watch she let out a gasp and jumped up. It was almost three o'clock; she was supposed to be down there by now.

Dropping the piano lid back into place she smoothed her skirt and ran her fingers through her hair, fanning it to create a bit more volume then grabbed her phone out of her handbag. Clicking onto the camera function she flicked it to forward facing and examined her lipstick. Good, it was still intact, she hadn't managed to bite it all off yet.

She had tried to get someone else to take her place but her pleas had gone unanswered. Everybody agreed she was the one who had to do it.

Arriving at the marquee a few minutes later Grace was shocked at the sea of people. Before she had slunk to the music room to gather her courage at least half the assembled chairs were empty. Now they were all occupied and there were people standing at the back.

What the hell?

Spying Sylvia at the edge of the stage she hurried over and pulled her aside. 'A *small* gathering you said?'

Sylvia shrugged. 'We thought it was. But apparently someone told the paper and then Channel 7 wanted to get on board. We couldn't say no to that kind of publicity.'

'There are TV cameras here?' Grace shrieked.

'Relax Grace, you can do this. Just think about it like reading a story, the very thing that brought you to Rosehill in the first place.'

Grace glared at her. 'Oh yeah, it's *totally* the same as that!'

Sylvia grabbed her hand and squeezed it tight. 'Grace you're fine. Remember who you're doing this for.'

'I'm not sure Edith would approve of emotional blackmail in her name.'

'You know she would.'

They were interrupted by the emcee. 'All right ladies, we need to get this show on the road.'

Grace shot a last imploring look at Sylvia. 'I really have to do this, don't I?'

Sylvia was already being led away to her position on the stage and could only give a thumbs up in response.

By the time it was her turn to speak Grace had managed to calm herself. Sylvia was right, she was essentially just reading a story and if she wanted the audience to truly appreciate the power of this particular story it was up to her to deliver it properly. Taking the three deep breaths her grandmother always insisted could diffuse any kind of stress, she gathered her notes and made her way to the podium.

'Good afternoon everyone and thank you so much for coming along to this very special event. As you can imagine the planning and development of our new wing was a lengthy and complex process and I am very proud to have been involved right from the concept phase. As Sylvia mentioned my name is Grace McDonald and I have worked here at Rosehill Gardens for the past two years. How that came to be is quite a long story but I will attempt to give you the abridged version as the real story I want to tell is about a lady named Edith who is the inspiration behind this amazing new facility right behind us here.'

Edith

It was funny how your name could define you in different ways.

Unlike most of her friends who hated the names their parents had lovingly bestowed upon them, Edith always felt privileged to be named after her great-grandmother, the first female to graduate from high school in the town of Wellings Bridge and an all-round formidable woman by all accounts.

It *was* an old fashioned name, even back when she was at school, but Edith liked the fact that it made her stand out in a positive way. Teachers never forgot her name and it was nice to know that there was not another Edith in the whole school.

It was a different story once she arrived at Rosehill though. There she was one of three Ediths, although of course she did have the distinction of being the youngest. By a full forty-five years.

Edith had not known that young people could end up in nursing homes. She had never contemplated what happened to thirty-three-year-olds who needed full time care and didn't have any family to look after them.

It seemed she wasn't alone in that regard. Her paperwork had been corrected by a helpful clerk somewhere along the application process, changing her year of birth from 1982 to 1932, and for the first full month she lived at Rosehill, *everybody* stared at her. Once they were on top of the uniqueness of her situation they went above and beyond any reasonable expectation in an effort to help her settle in. But still, it was never a situation that she was going to be excited about.

The colourful walls and bedding that so boldly defined Edith at Rosehill were ironic really as she had always preferred neutral shades. But upon realising that Room 46 was to be her home possibly forever she had been overcome by an overwhelming desire to protest and luminous colours were the best she could come up with. The one exception had been Joe's old chair. It had to stay exactly as he had left it although they certainly would have fixed the springs and re-covered it had she asked.

At least she had still been able to speak then. It was hard to fathom how different her time at Rosehill might have been if she had not been able to communicate verbally right from the start.

The speaking was the other great irony. Edith was by nature an introvert. Teaching had forced her to find her voice and use it, but that was more playing a role and something that could be switched on just for the classroom. Anybody who knew her before the accident would have described her as quiet and unassuming. So, it was only when her voice was the only thing she had that she started using more than she ever had before. Maybe it was because she subconsciously knew she had such a limited time left to communicate verbally.

Some days Edith woke up feeling as if she had lost forty years of her life, that she had skipped from relative youth to old age without any of the great memories or experiences that should accompany that transition. It wasn't that she didn't like and respect old people, she certainly did, and had actually made many senior citizen friends when she and Joe had been on their road trip. They had even joked about being honorary grey nomads. It had felt like being the butt of the cruellest joke when Edith had been told what her care options were after the first stroke.

Of course nobody was insensitive enough to ask her what she missed most about her old life but if they had she could have named dozens of things. Hands down her darling Joe was top of the list. The seven years they had spent together were just a glorious memory now, a sacred space she allowed herself to visit every morning and evening. She didn't doubt he was with her still and knew it was he who had secured her place at Rosehill. But it was hard to understand why he couldn't have stopped the second stroke that robbed her of her voice and really sealed her fate.

Almost as devastating was the loss of movement and, therefore, the ability to go where she wanted when she wanted. Nor could she cook her own meals, go to the cinema, drive a car, drink a real coffee, swim in the ocean, ride a bike ... the list was literally endless. When she remembered how she used to complain about the rowdy boys in 8E or the horrible girls in her Year Nine class, she couldn't believe how shallow those problems seemed now, how easy to solve.

It was Sylvia who had suggested the reading volunteers. The two women were much the same age and Edith was touched by how hard Sylvia tried to make her life at Rosehill as fulfilling as possible. The first few months she spent there they had shared many late afternoon chats, discovering they had a lot in common. Both were the only child of a single parent, although Sylvia knew her father but

Edith didn't. Uncannily both had lost their mothers to breast cancer when they were in their late twenties. Learning how much Edith loved reading and storytelling Sylvia immediately put her on the roster, promising she would send the most interesting volunteers her way.

It had been a bit of a motley crew that had done their stint in Room 46 and once she had written the stories Edith no longer thought of them by their real names, only the fictional ones she had bestowed on them. They had all seemed happy with their alter egos as none had asked her to change them.

Sarah was on the tail end of her community service when she arrived at Rosehill whereas Jake was just starting his. Edith found it amusing that he had signed up for community service voluntarily but certainly respected the moral compass that was directing him to repent for his previous unsavoury deeds. Bev and Audrey had come via a community organisation encouraging people at a loose end on the weekend to volunteer somewhere and Margaret did it in memory of her mother who had spent her last few years at Rosehill Gardens. Josephine was there for more practical reasons. She had a financial stake in the facility and wanted an anonymous way to check the running of the place without giving the staff an opportunity to be on their best behaviour.

Edith had been surprised at how willingly they all shared their own stories. She wasn't sure if it was to humour a person they felt sorry for or if it was just because that despite what most people said they did like to talk about themselves.

Grace's arrival at Rosehill impacted Edith more than she expected. It had felt surreal to have someone so young reading and discussing stories with her, making her feel like a teacher again. The fact she was reading Edith's own stories also gave her an interesting perspective on what she had written. Having always harboured a secret dream to write a book one day, she couldn't believe it had taken such a life-changing event to make it happen. She had always told her students that the best way to really appreciate a story was to hear it read aloud, although she had never expected just how that point would be proved to her.

She and Sylvia had come up with the post story discussion as a way to build Grace's confidence, but Edith had found it to be just as beneficial for her as for the younger woman. It had surprised her too just how much she pitied Grace. She had not felt anything beyond self-pity since the accident and it was comforting on some level that she still possessed the ability to feel sorry for somebody else.

The decision to record the story without Grace's permission wasn't one they had made lightly but both she and Sylvia had felt such a driving need to help. It had saddened her beyond all measure that Grace had left that day in such distress and that she hadn't had the opportunity to see her again and make things right before her last day there.

Marion

Although not part of the staff delegation seated up the front, Marion wouldn't have missed the official opening of the new wing for anything. So many things had happened since that auspicious day she had come across Grace's paperwork on Sylvia's desk, most of all the assuaging of her own guilt.

Marion thought back to the day at Strauss Academy when she handed in the packet of pills to Saskia Van der Linden. Thinking she was just doing her job, she had not expected the principal to react so severely. And more devastatingly, neither did she expect that young Grace McDonald would take off the way she did. It was one of those days she wished she could rewind and start again.

With hindsight she wouldn't have swapped the cleaning days of the east and west blocks or broken her iron clad rule of not moving a student's personal belongings. She would have dusted around the precarious mound of textbooks on Grace's desk instead of rescuing them from what she felt was imminent collapse onto the collection of mugs and plates on the floor. Most definitely, she would have listened to the little voice that was telling her that exams were almost over and there was probably no harm done.

Yes, Marion had tried to make amends and had set in motion a fair measure of damage control. She had planted the idea that Grace's parents might look for media attention or even sue the school if Ms Van der Linden opted to withhold Grace's school results. The principal had not admitted to this line of thought but Marion knew her well enough to predict this as a possible course of action. Furthermore, she had assured Ms Van der Linden that the education department didn't need to know that Grace hadn't actually attended her last term of school. Given that all her academic work had been completed it was only a technicality anyway.

She had stayed at the school long enough to make sure Grace did officially graduate from Strauss (at least on paper), then moved on to a new job, convincing long serving secretary Beryl Adams that she should apply for a new position as well. Although the loss of two key staff members would not actually help Grace, Marion did take a small degree of satisfaction at leaving Saskia Van der Linden spectacularly in the lurch right at the beginning of a school year.

Looking up at the animated young woman on the stage, Marion couldn't quite decipher what she felt. Pride certainly, but still a trace of guilt and a huge amount of gratitude that like most office workers, the students at Strauss never saw the cleaners who tended to their rooms.

In the years since the whole incident, Marion had done her best to come to terms with her conscience. She had even sought professional help after she started to obsess about what had happened to Grace. The best case scenario was that the young woman had eventually found her way back home and had rejoiced when her Senior Certificate and OP statement turned up in the letterbox like every other graduate. The worst case scenario had Marion imagining Grace falling into prostitution to support a drug habit or some other unsavoury situation.

'You were just doing your job Marion,' her psychologist Paula had assured her numerous times. 'You had no way of knowing what the outcome would be. Didn't you tell me your code of conduct required you to report anything drug related that you came across no matter how minor?'

'Yes, but…'

'No buts Marion, it simply wasn't your call. Ultimately, Saskia and Grace both over-reacted to something that, all things being fair, should have been sorted out fairly easily.'

Marion had eventually accepted Paula's advice and moved on with her life. Leaving the contract cleaning company she had been temping with since her departure from Strauss, she applied for the job at Rosehill. She had been there a year when Edith moved in.

Sylvia had pulled her aside and informed her that she alone would be cleaning Edith's room. 'I just think it would be better to have only one person working in there, given how delicate the situation is,' she said, leaving Marion to read between the lines.

Not that the other cleaners minded.

'I seriously couldn't handle it,' Zindzi confessed. 'It would just freak me out to think that can happen to someone so young.'

Matheus revealed that he suffered from paranoia and couldn't stand anybody watching him work. And, suddenly petrified that she too might suffer a stroke, Hazel went out on stress leave.

Marion and Edith had become good friends during the first few months when she could speak, a friendship that continued on into the more difficult times after she lost her speech. Learning so much about the young woman through their regular chats, Marion had done what she could to improve Edith's quality of life.

Of course it had to be done through official channels, which was why she always cleaned Sylvia's office at 8.15 am. The assistant manager always came in a half an hour early to prepare for her day and as unobtrusively as possible Marion always managed to drop what she believed to be relevant information into the brief conversations they shared.

One day she mentioned she was going to bring in some talking books because Edith loved to read. Another day she commented on the piece on *Sixty Minutes* about the amazing iPad apps that existed these days. Yet another time she said how sad it was that Edith would never realise her ambition to become a writer. Marion had also convinced her own hairdresser to visit Edith twice a week as her way of giving back to the community.

Despite Sylvia receiving the credit for these ideas, Marion bore no malice. In fact, she was happy enough that they came to fruition at all. She was enough of a pragmatist to accept that while being a cleaner might have educated her far better than any university degree could, the people who ruled the world and its institutions were never going to come to her for advice. Therefore, she had to pitch her ideas to them without them realising who was really steering the boat.

Grace

The nerves she had experienced earlier were largely forgotten as her speech gathered steam. Grace had hit her stride and she could see how involved the audience were with the story. For the first time she realised that everybody hadn't just been trying to make her feel better, she really did seem to have a knack for storytelling.

'We were all devastated to lose Edith from Rosehill,' she said. 'For the first few months we just tried to get on with things but eventually we realised that even though she was no longer with us, we had to do something about creating a dedicated wing for young people in full time care. While Edith was the only non-senior resident who has ever lived here at Rosehill, there are hundreds of younger people living in various aged care facilities around the country, simply because they have no other choices.

'As you can imagine, funding was our greatest challenge. We did all the usual things to raise funds and a few less usual things too but it was the bequests of two former Rosehill residents that finally got the ball rolling. And throughout the whole process Edith has remained foremost in our thoughts.'

Grace paused and stepped back from the podium to allow a short video to play, honouring the two philanthropist residents whose monetary gifts had kick started the campaign to build the Young Care wing at Rosehill. Blinking back tears she did her best to maintain her composure upon seeing Doris and Archie on the big screen. She had known both of them and remained touched beyond words that they had helped this amazing project happen by the bequests they left in their wills.

Waiting for the applause to die down, she stepped

forward again to continue speaking. 'While Doris and Archie's gifts were massive, we don't have the luxury of resting on our laurels,' she said. 'As you can see, the facility is built and fitted out and we will welcome our first residents next week. But to keep this special wing running and give the residents within all the very best therapies available we need more money.

'I know, I know, there are thousands of worthy causes out there so that is why we are not merely asking for donations. Of course if you would like to donate we won't hold you back, but we have a couple of ventures happening which will get you some bang for your buck. The first of these is Edith's book, *Observations From Room 46*, which will be available over to the left of the marquee after the official part of this afternoon is over.'

A murmur ran around the marquee at this announcement and most of the crowd turned to see the impressive display that had just been unveiled with a huge banner featuring the book cover and stacks of paperbacks on the table below. Once again Grace fought back tears. If only Edith was here to see it, she thought sadly. She caught Sylvia's eye and could see the other woman was having the same thought.

'If you didn't come prepared today to purchase a copy, they will be available from the main office right here at Rosehill, from all good bookstores and as an ebook download from all the major digital sellers. In addition to Edith's book, I and several of my classmates from the UQ School of Music will be running full day musical appreciation workshops for children of all ages over the upcoming school holiday break. At twenty dollars for the day, we think it is amazing value and every cent will go towards the Young Care Wing. Please take a flier and let as many people know about it as you can.

'Finally as an ongoing fundraiser, the students at Edith's old school Baker College will run a sausage sizzle and coffee stand every Saturday from now on at the Southside Farmers Markets. If you are ever in the area they would love your support.'

Another round of applause sounded, giving Grace an opportunity to sneak a swig from her water bottle. She'd been fighting an annoying tickle in her throat for the past few minutes and was glad of the chance to quell it before she continued speaking.

'Thank you so much for coming along today and being involved in the opening of our Young Care wing. It is a very exciting day and we are overjoyed that this project has come to fruition. In saying that though we can't help feeling just a little bit sad too. This is Edith's day and by rights she should be here to be a part of it. Sadly that was just not meant to be but thanks to the wonders of modern technology you can still send her your support. If you can all please turn to the right and look up you will see a camera. On the count of three when the red light flashes can we all give Edith a big wave.'

Grace waited a moment while everyone got into position then leaned back down to the microphone. 'Okay ready one, two, three, wave…'

Edith

Edith smiled thankfully as the nurse rearranged her pillows to let her sit up a little. She was still so weak, but definitely starting to improve baby step by baby step. It was hard to read the nurse's expression behind the facemask, but her eyes were bright and lively. Clapping her hands excitedly she reached onto her trolley and triumphantly held up Edith's iPad, which was wrapped in clear, sterile plastic. Edith smiled again, delighted to have her link to the outside world back. In truth she had been too sick the past week to even look at it, but she had still felt bereft without it.

The nurse set the tablet up on the table and used a gloved finger to turn it on and navigate to the live streaming app. She chattered brightly, clearly as excited as Edith to watch the broadcast. Edith caught a few words, but her brain was still too fuzzy to concentrate properly. She had made an effort to learn some Russian phrases before she came but was struggling to recall them at this point in time.

She watched excitedly as the screen came to life, pixelating for a moment before coming back into focus. Edith's breath caught in her throat as she watched Grace step up to the podium and begin to speak.

* * * * *

It had amazed Edith just how arbitrary the decision was that had taken her from Rosehill. One extra tick on a spreadsheet and she was in the next care bracket, and suddenly the staff who had looked after her so well were deemed no longer competent to continue with her care. The new place was attached to a private hospital with a specialist stroke wing. Everything was state of the art, clean and sterile and she had a higher ratio of carers with more of them being at the RN level. Physically she had the best care possible but mentally she threw in the towel. The drive and courage that had gotten her through those horrible months after the accident and the loss of Joe and that had sustained her throughout the time she lived at Rosehill finally deserted her.

Due to the limited daytime only visiting hours it was difficult for the staff from Rosehill to visit. They came when they could, but not nearly enough to sustain Edith through the rest of the long, lonely days and weeks. She accepted all the drugs that were offered and refused offers to eat meals in the dining room or to participate in other social activities. She could see how shocked Sylvia and Grace were at her deterioration but just didn't have the strength to fight any more. It *had* pleased Edith to see the change in Grace, but not enough to lift the fog of despair that she had sunk into.

It had taken a lot of negotiation and even more paperwork to allow Edith to be transported back to Rosehill twice a week to take part in the newly instigated music therapy program Grace had set up. It had been another one of Sylvia's ideas, triggered by watching a documentary about stroke victims who could sing even though they couldn't speak.

In the first few sessions, Edith had just gone through the motions, not knowing any of the old time songs the other residents loved and still too cushioned by her medication to connect with what was happening around her. But over time she slowly came around. The regular trips away from her care facility were diversions, and a step outside the very small universe she now occupied. Hearing the songs over and over again helped her learn the words and soon she couldn't help but participate. At first she couldn't believe it was actually her voice she was hearing – a little raspy to begin with but as strong and sure as it had ever been as time went on. She wasn't what you might call a talented singer but she had a fair voice as good as any of the others in the room.

At first the changes were too small to really notice but gradually they started becoming more significant.

* * * * *

'It was so exciting to see the changes in Edith,' Grace said. 'Especially for me. Remember, I had never heard her speak, so to actually hear her voice in song for the first time was just amazing.'

A soft murmur ran around the audience, with many people nodding their heads and smiling at this announcement. Grace smiled too, while doing her best not to look at the television camera that was now trained directly on her.

'It wasn't a miracle cure by any means,' she continued, 'but things definitely started to happen. As has been known to happen in many cases, Edith regained some of her speech and her general mood and concentration also picked up. Within nine weeks she had improved enough to come back to Rosehill. Once we had her back with us I really stepped things up and spent an hour every day after work trying all the techniques available.'

Grace paused for a moment, centring herself so as to keep her emotions in check and her voice steady.

'To watch Edith slowly claw her way back to limited speech and some movement was the most humbling thing I have ever experienced. Sure she still needed full time care, but the quality of her life improved beyond all expectation. And then one day Edith finally caught the lucky break she so sorely deserved.'

* * * * *

Edith hadn't realised she was crying until she felt her nurse dabbing her cheeks with a tissue. 'Are you all right?' she asked in her heavily accented English.

Edith managed a weary smile. 'Yes,' she murmured. 'Happy.'

'Okay,' the nurse replied, her eyes studying Edith carefully all the same.

It still felt surreal to be in a hospital ward in Russia. Edith and Joe had talked about visiting Russia and she felt so sad that he wasn't there to enjoy it with her, limited cultural experience as it was.

Edith had been warned the chemotherapy drugs were the worst part of the stem cell treatment but given all that she had endured in the past few years she thought she would take it in her stride. The reality was that nothing could have prepared her for the onslaught.

When her friends at Rosehill had initially planned the date of the official opening and Edith's book launch, they had thought she would be home and hopefully well enough to take some part in proceedings. But they hadn't counted on the setbacks. First there was the scheduling mistake which saw her treatment start date bumped back a month, and then came the life threatening infection that left her in isolation for a further fortnight. But now things seemed to be finally looking up.

With a bit of luck she would have the procedure the following week.

It was just as well she was fortunate enough to have some cash in reserve.

* * * * *

The issue of compensation was something Edith didn't dwell on. While she knew a payment would eventually come her way, she had been warned it could take years as the insurance companies fought it out between themselves and all relevant evidence was gathered and examined. With Joe dead and her having such a limited ability to communicate, getting their side of the story across was always going to be a protracted affair.

Edith had been shocked to awaken from a nap one afternoon to see a distinguished gentleman in an Armani suit seated in Joe's chair. Looking up from the stack of documents in his lap he smiled and nodded politely. Edith blinked to clear her vision. Although the reading volunteers came in all shapes and sizes, she'd never had a dapper man in a suit before.

Self-conscious about the way her voice sounded she tried her hardest to speak clearly. 'Not reading day,' she mumbled.

'Oh no, I'm not here to read,' the man explained with a

warm smile. 'Trust me you'd be back asleep in seconds. I was always the worst in my class at reading aloud. My name is Edward Collins from Collins, Barrett and Wilson Solicitors. I'm here to work on your compensation claim.'

It turned out that Edward was the son of one of Rosehill's residents. Always careful to be utterly professional Sylvia could not be accused of using her position to acquire Edward's professional services. But there was nothing unethical about having him visit his mother during music therapy, ensuring Edith was in his line of vision and giving detailed answers to his questions as to why she was there.

At first Edith had been a little taken aback at Edward's forthright manner and the almost clinical way he asked questions. She still found it hard to talk about Joe, but Edward didn't cut her any slack, eliciting every last skerrick of information about Joe's life and untimely death. Then just when she was at the point of breaking down in tears Edward had surprised her with a warm hug.

'I know it's hard,' he said with genuine empathy, 'but to the other driver's insurance company Joe is not the kind, funny and loving husband you lost, he is a an amount, a financial loss on their balance sheet. My job is to make them pay and pay dearly for your loss and the only way I can do that is to prove the kind of life he was destined to live before their client ignored a stop sign on a rainy afternoon.'

Edith had been amazed how swiftly Edward managed to get the wheels in motion and was absolutely floored at the sum awarded to her. Sylvia had turned down her offer to donate some of it to the Young Care wing. 'That's your money

232

Edith,' she had said firmly. 'Use it to get the best of care for yourself. We'll work out a way to raise what we need here.'

Three months later she was on a plane to Russia.

* * * * *

When the audience turned to wave at Edith the tears flowed freely. And this time the nurse had to wipe her own tears away before tending to her patient.

Marion

The applause at the end of Grace's presentation was long and loud. Marion clapped until her hands hurt, happy beyond all measure to see Grace standing in front of an audience and if not actually confident then doing a great job of acting like she was. She could see Grace's family seated up near the front, their faces glowing with pride. Her mother and sister were wiping away tears.

Since those first hesitant days in Room 46 Grace had come so far. She had completed the usual Aged Care training and cut her teeth as a Personal Carer before moving into her specialised role. And this past year she had even enrolled part time at uni, dipping her toe back in the water and taking her first steps on the road towards maybe becoming a performer. Marion couldn't help but feel proud of that.

It had always been Marion's aim to have Grace set up a music therapy program at Rosehill, right from the day she saw the Centrelink papers on Sylvia's desk. But the whole venture had taken some doing. She hadn't realised just how worn down Grace was nor how far she had removed herself from the musical circles she used to occupy.

There is no magic cure for anxiety and the rebuilding of a broken spirit, but time, therapy and a positive purpose in life had certainly gotten Grace back on the straight and narrow. She was one of the fortunate ones though, having a team of people who supported her each step of the way. And of course being assigned to Rosehill in the first place was a major lucky break.

Marion was ashamed to admit she had once been quite unsympathetic of those on welfare. Having worked hard all her life she had no time for those who seemed to simply not want to find a job. Sure, there were some who cheated the system but she had come to realise there were certainly many more who had simply fallen between the cracks.

As much as she loved working at Rosehill Gardens Marion considered it might be time to move on. Knowing so many people in the industry it wouldn't be difficult to get a job cleaning the office of her local federal Member of Parliament and at the Community Access Centre just down the road. Now she had some firm ideas about how people could be encouraged back to work as opposed to simply being forced off welfare, it was up to her to get them into the ears of those who could do something about it.

Joining the lengthy queue to purchase a copy of Edith's book Marion caught a glimpse of Sylvia and Grace being interviewed by a Channel 7 reporter. Seeing the camaraderie between the two and the animated and passionate way Grace was speaking finally dislodged the heaviness in her chest that had become so ingrained that she had simply become used to carrying it around.

For so long Marion had been weighed down at the realisation her actions had quite possibly ruined a young woman's life, but now, finally, she was starting to see the bigger picture.

Marion was as much in the dark as the next person as to why things happened in life exactly as they did, but right here and right now she suddenly had the sense that everything was exactly as it should be.

Epilogue

Josephine closed her copy of *Observations From Room 46* and set it down on the old stool she used as a coffee table. Sylvia had provided her with a complimentary copy along with a nice note gently suggesting that a donation equivalent to the purchase price would be very welcome. At the time Josephine had brushed the suggestion aside, the same way she always did when people asked her for money. But after actually reading the book she felt a tiny frisson of discomfiture.

No, that wasn't right – it was more like a stab to the solar plexus.

Josephine couldn't fault the book and the way it was written and Edith had certainly kept her word about changing the details enough so nobody would know the first story was about her. The problem was that *she* knew and as of this moment it was not something she felt good about.

It was one of those defining moments like an overweight person seeing an unflattering photograph of themselves or a "happy drunk" witnessing their outrageous antics on video.

Josephine finally saw herself as others did.

Determined to banish the unsettling thoughts from her mind, Josephine went on her customary Saturday afternoon walk. She would never set foot inside a gym and had always shaken her head at the idea of paying to use an indoor space when the great outdoors was there to use free of charge. It hadn't stopped her investing in a company that leased gym equipment but that was different. Business was business. Right?

Frustratingly, the walk only served to make her mind more active rather than quietening it down. Suddenly the way she lived her life didn't make complete sense any more.

The unwelcome self-analysis continued as she ate dinner and sat down to watch TV. Perhaps it was a little bit silly to re-watch a movie she had already seen four times rather than buying herself a DVD player. People were always selling them for peanuts at garage sales and you could borrow movies from the library. And maybe it was time to see if her local op shop had a more suitable TV, preferably one that didn't cut the edges off everything because of its compact screen size.

Feeling more unsettled than she could ever remember, Josephine banished the book to the very bottom of her wardrobe and went to bed. But sleep simply wouldn't come and amidst much tossing and turning she finally admitted to herself just how uncomfortable her thirty-year-old bed really was.

The first light of dawn found Josephine sitting at the kitchen table with her chequebook open. *Observations From Room 46* had been retrieved during the long, lonely night and she had re-read her story several times, each time leading her to the same conclusion.

She would have to shuffle some cash around, but that could be done first thing Monday morning, well before the cheque would arrive by courier on Tuesday. It was a company cheque issued from a private trust fund that was untraceable to her directly. Her signature was illegible enough to further conceal her identity.

Josephine certainly did not want any publicity. She was

not going to advertise to the public that she had the means to give sizeable donations and she would hate that those who knew of her in the business community might think she was losing her sharp edge.

It was actually more of a financial strategy than an emotional response, she decided as she carefully copied the fundraising account name from the back page of Edith's book on to the payee line of the cheque. Last year she had paid a fortune in tax so this would reduce her next tax bill considerably.

As much as she rationalised it away as a business decision, Josephine's hand still shook a little as she wrote out the amount.

One million dollars.

About The Author

Helen McKenna lives on the Sunshine Coast in Queensland. She has a Bachelor of Arts degree from the University of Queensland and has worked in banking, local government and learning support and currently works as a biographer and swimming teacher.

Room 46 is her second novel.

Also by Helen McKenna:

The Beach House
The Perfect Proposal (short story)
Flashback (short stories)

How Do I Write My Life Story?

Contact:

Email: info@helenmckenna.com.au
Website: www.helenmckenna.com.au
Facebook: www.facebook.com/HelenMcKenna.Author
Twitter: www.twitter.com/helenmckenna_